NOELENE

HEARTBREAK COUNTRY

Complete and Unabridged

AURORA
Leicester

First published in 2020

First Aurora Edition
published 2021

A catalogue record for this book is available
from the British Library.

ISBN 978–1–78782–663–2

Published by
Ulverscroft Limited
Anstey, Leicestershire

Printed and bound in Great Britain by
TJ Books Ltd., Padstow, Cornwall

This book is printed on acid-free paper

1

As she knelt by the grave, Tilly Schroder let fat salty tears drizzle down her cheeks. Five years ago, she buried her fiancé, Christian Hunter, and their baby daughter together.

She arranged the last of her Ma's sweet peas, ranunculus and daisies from the farmhouse garden, then tucked great frothy white bunches of baby's breath and tiny spikes of rosemary in around the edges of the flower container. For remembrance. Not that she could ever forget. That fateful night was seared into her memory.

The heavy emotions of this anniversary day in early spring always surfaced strong and deep. As part of her silent grieving process, she opened the usually closed prison walls of her heart and set them free.

Focusing on gathering together her scissors, bucket and water bottle, Tilly suffered anew the ongoing emptiness of her private grief that she hoped one day to overcome. That her sapping sorrow might ease, to be replaced with only memories of a beautiful short-lived love and happier times.

Deep in thoughts, both fond and sad, she paused in her weeping when an inexplicable instinct slowly crept in. An awareness of another presence. The crunch of a footfall on the nearby gravel path that edged the rows, then a shadow that fell across the grave jolted her attention into sharper focus and her senses more alive.

A fellow mourner and local paying their respects perhaps? She looked and felt a mess but didn't care. Confused from grieving, she slowly turned to identify her company.

At first sight of the visitor, Tilly reeled in shock and rose abruptly to her feet. He looked mean, as always. A grim sour expression on his wrinkled face. Unshaven and with bloodshot eyes, his breath reeking of alcohol, it was clear he was already on the drink. But when was he ever sober?

As horrified recognition registered in her clearing brain, it also took note of the rifle slung carelessly under his arm and pointed loosely in her direction.

She wisely assumed it was loaded and knew exactly why he was here. It wasn't for any social niceties. In his world it was all about intimidation and bullying.

Tilly swallowed hard and clenched her hands together to still their trembling. Not from fear but a deep unceasing anger and mistrust. All the same, just in case, she took a cautionary step backward. Pain had long since hardened her heart against this excuse for a man, unworthy of her compassion on so many fronts.

Yes, he had lost a son that day. His fault, not hers. And yes, only weeks prior, he had lost his wife in a tragic farm accident. But even the law overruled his emotional pleas for leniency.

And today was probably one of his first days of freedom after what should have been a five year incarceration. Tilly frowned. It seemed too soon for his release. By her calculation, surely he

2

should have served another six or twelve months. Unless the dangerous little weasel had talked his way to a sentence reduction. It wouldn't be for good behaviour.

'Joe.'

When he smirked she wanted to reach out and slap his face so hard he fell over. But for now, since he held a rifle, had the upper hand and knew it, her caution slowly edged toward alarm and she held her breath.

'I'll git you for what you did,' he growled like an animal about to launch into its prey.

Tilly wondered if that meant now. This minute. And her first helpless thoughts flew to her mother. There wasn't another soul for miles around nor was there likely to be. Unbelievable that the bastard's standard reflex action was always to blame another when he was at fault.

'You went to prison for a reason,' she said dryly, faking a confidence she didn't feel.

'It was all your fault.' He hitched the gun higher and his finger played with the trigger.

Stay calm. Be cool. He's baiting you. Don't react. She repeated the words in her head like a mantra.

Tilly didn't intend to waste words on him. If he planned on doing her harm, let him get on with it. This close, wherever he hit was going to hurt. Meanwhile the mongrel would never see reason. Not his crusty nature.

When her side vision caught movement further across the cemetery Tilly tried not to look too obvious and squinted over his shoulder. She hoped the fact that she wore sunglasses helped hide her distraction and side glance. Beneath the gently swaying tops of the box eucalypts bordering the cemetery perimeter in a far corner, an unfamiliar heavily bearded man emerged from behind a gnarled tree trunk.

A drifter? Probably a lost nomadic soul wandering the bush countryside as he pleased. Yet he seemed to be deliberately staring in their direction. For a moment, Tilly wildly wondered whether to raise an arm and call out for help but there was no need. Her heart beat even faster, this time in hope, as he began to stride with determined purpose toward them.

A ragged old hat was tugged down low over his face so that it was barely visible. As he moved closer she saw enough to notice a scowling haunted expression but little more. The man's approach was stealthy until he reached the gravel path and seemed to deliberately make a point of creating noise as a diversion.

It worked.

Joe whipped around, the rifle swinging wildly along with him, but before he could speak the newcomer said in a deep controlled voice. 'Turn it on me, old man, but leave the woman alone.'

Who was this scruffy derelict person speaking with such conviction? Potentially prepared to take a bullet in her place?

'Git out of my sight,' Joe growled.

To Tilly it sounded like he knew the stranger.

'I can take you on and you know it.' He stood cool and unflinching, staring Joe down. 'Put it on safety and back off.'

Amazingly, perhaps unsettled by his younger

4

and stronger challenger, Joe awkwardly shuffled and said in a voice that no longer held its former authority, 'You'll keep. I'm back to stay.'

'Not if you use that thing.' The newcomer nodded toward the rifle.

'Watch your step. Both of you,' the old man called over his shoulder as he staggered back along the path to the cemetery entrance.

Immediately Joe had moved on, the Good Samaritan said, 'Are you all right?'

Close up the man was probably younger than he looked. If he shaved off that forest covering his face he might look half decent. His lean body looked underfed. Not a spare inch of flesh on his bones. Yet despite giving the impression of being down and out, he held a mobile phone in one hand.

'Miss?'

How could he know she was single? Fair enough, there was no ring on her left hand but that wasn't a given these days. Yet the tone of his quietly uttered probe came as a surprise. What happened, she wondered, that a man of some manners was clearly friends with hardship? And why would a complete stranger care enough about a sad woman in a cemetery to get involved in a dangerous situation?

Too emotionally shaken from her grieving and Joe's frightening appearance, Tilly nodded. 'I'll be fine. Thank you.' Although his arrival was timely, why was she troubled with a feeling that this wasn't by coincidence? 'You don't live around here.' It wasn't a question. She knew everyone in the district.

He shook his head.

'Just passing through then?'

He nodded. Why was he reluctant to speak?

'Sounded like he knew you.'

He paused and lifted his broad shoulders in a shrug. 'Your typical drunken old timer.'

Tilly noted he hadn't answered her question. After a long day in the classroom, exhaustion from a day of renewed annual grieving and a sickening encounter with Joe Hunter, she was beat. She didn't have the energy to push further and was unlikely to see this man again. Weird how some people only briefly touched your life yet left a lasting impact.

Not knowing why she felt any concern or interest in this wretched specimen of a human being, her compassion rose to the fore. She wasn't heartless. She had raised baby animals, chickens, puppies and kittens; nursed the weakest lambs back to health and rescued orphaned joeys from the bush. Living on the land all her life, the sense of mateship and country hospitality that sat innately deep and powerful in her soul kicked into play.

'If you're looking to camp, it's private land all around here but down beyond that boundary fence and line of trees,' she pointed east across the flat paddocks lush with green grain crops and flowering golden canola, 'is the swamp nature reserve. Still has a slow flow of running water in Reedy Creek. And it's sheltered.'

He waited awhile before muttering, 'Obliged.'

He didn't immediately leave, just lingered, wandering away among the oldest gravestones on the far side of the central gravel pathway opposite the lawn section leaving a frowning Tilly staring after him.

It wasn't until she finally walked back to her vehicle and drove away that she glanced in the rear view mirror to see the man saunter back over to where she had just been in the cemetery. Checking to see who she had been visiting today? Why would he bother when he wouldn't know them?

* * *

As always at this time of year, he had waited and watched for Tilly Schroder, knowing without fail she would appear. He had always remained out of sight but when he recognised the predatory man who appeared, a fierce sense of urgency and protection filled his gut.

Joe Hunter was notoriously irrational and unpredictable. His appearance could have meant life or death. He had no choice but to intervene. The old man had recognised him and, at one point, he wondered if Tilly may have picked up on it, too. No surprise if she didn't. The years hadn't particularly treated him bad but, all the same, he knew every time he looked in a cracked motel mirror he had definitely changed.

Grief had always been a part of the reason for his return. Tilly's own heartache clearly still strong. But family shame over Joe's drunken irresponsible actions that night left him frustrated and angry, wishing he could just turn back the clock.

He was amused and touched when Tilly suggested their old camping place down by the creek. And yeah, she was just as beautiful as the day he last saw her, same time last year and every year around this time for the past four years. Nothing in the world felt like coming home.

He haunted the Bingun cemetery like a living ghost until she arrived, hungry to grab a glimpse of the woman who had taken his breath away since he was a gawky teenager. Not that Tilly Schroder would ever be his. But a man could dream. He always knew he would die for her. Today that circumstance almost came true.

As children, all through primary and secondary, they had ridden on the school bus together every day. Although once they hit their teens it was clear that Tilly only had eyes for another. So he could only look on from afar and wish life had turned out differently for them all.

Returning like he did was a kind of torture but he needed to reassure himself that Tilly was okay. He hurt in anguish along with her to witness how much she still endured a crushing grief, kneeling before that ominous grave, head bowed, not moving for quite some time.

He usually watched from afar, aching to comfort her. But he resisted. Until today when forced to emerge, his heart pounding hard in fear at the potentially deadly situation. To save her. See her almost close enough to touch.

But where this year was just the same for Tilly Schroder, this year for him would be different. This year he planned to stay.

He bowed his head in respect before the same grave Tilly had knelt only a few moments ago, before he cheekily removed one of Mrs. Schroder's finest blooms from its beautiful arrangement to go place it on another lonely grave nearby. It angered him that it still bore no proper headstone which he aimed to change now he was back.

Then he strode for the trees along the fence to retrieve his swag and headed to the familiar camping spot down by the creek.

★ ★ ★

Tilly flicked on the blinker and turned into Swamp Road, so named for the low wetland area further down to which she had directed the stranger at the cemetery. It flooded over winter, attracting ducks and pelicans, and lay at the bottom of the gently sloping home paddock below the Schroder farmhouse.

As she turned in at their farm gate, Isla ran to greet her. Tilly stopped the car to check the mailbox and while the door was open, the Sheltie leapt inside. Her sweet-faced pet was a tri colour, mostly black with splashes of sable, a white chest and feet.

'Cheeky girl,' Tilly fondly scolded when she climbed back into the car, stroking the dog who had taken up her usual position on the front passenger seat.

Owning Isla, who had been a puppy engagement gift from Christian, was bittersweet. They were going to create a home. Man, woman, child and their first family pet. She loved the beautiful faithful dog but it also reminded her daily of what she had lost. The engagement ring she had received the same day still sat in its royal blue velvet box at the very back of one of the dresser drawers in her room. A taunting vision of what might have been.

In the late afternoon, shaking aside her heavy thoughts impossible to avoid on this day, Tilly drove on along the gum-lined driveway, the lowering sun glinting through their topmost leaves. She pulled up outside the white timber house gate by its enclosing paling fence. Her mother's prolific flowering spring garden was rampant with colour and varieties, the vegetable paddock around the side a testament to Stella's hard work.

The orchard beyond was a vision of foamy pink and white blossom from peach, apricot and plum trees along with citrus and apples. Grape and passionfruit vines scrambled at either ends of the fence. The bounty the farm produced always meant the freezer and pantry were fully stocked with giveaways readily handed out all year.

Isla romped excitedly around her as Tilly walked up the steps and around the side built-in veranda that now formed a utility room off the substantial farmhouse kitchen. Coats hung on wall hooks and boots placed neatly on a rack beneath. She offloaded her cemetery supplies and sniffed the aroma of Ma's casserole that drew her toward the heart of their home.

The double gas stove had replaced the old wood IXL but an open fire silently pushed out its warmth at the far end living area. Wide windows took in the peaceful country views, green after good winter rains. The surrounding farm paddocks were sown to grains and legumes, the flowering canola almost as high as the fence and spreading squares of stunning yellow at intervals across the landscape.

Isla settled herself in front of the fire and Tilly made a start on chopping the vegetables, grateful for some time alone to recover from the nasty cemetery encounter with Joe that had left her shaken.

If the stranger hadn't arrived, the outcome could have been entirely different. Tilly refused to dwell on the threatening incident and waited for Ma to return from the garden. She practically lived out there, puddling all day and only reluctantly conceding at dusk to come inside.

Tonight, however, her mother appeared earlier than usual, hanging up her garden apron and tools and washing up in the laundry before trotting through to the kitchen.

She would be livid to know Joe Hunter was already released and back in the community. His wife, Alice, had been Ma's lifelong friend and neighbour.

Stella marched into the kitchen, her grey curly hair windblown, weather-beaten skin lightly tanned all year from the outdoor life she loved. Almost as tall as her daughter, wiry, straight-backed, forthright in voicing any opinion, her Ma was also blessed with the kindest heart of any person Tilly knew.

They exchanged smiles. 'How was your day?'

'Barrowed up and spread manure. Might take

a run into town tomorrow for trays of seedlings.'

Stella Harwich had only met and married Carl Schroder in middle age, the reason Tilly was an only child. They had lost the quietly hardworking man of the house and anchor of their small family three years ago, leased out the farmland to local agricultural contractors and the two women now rubbed along companionably together.

Knowing her daughter had been to the cemetery and darting a perceptive side glance toward her visible shreds of distress, Stella quietly asked, 'Are you all right, dear?'

Tilly nodded and, weirdly, remembered the stranger's similar words. A vision of him returned to mind and she frowned. She also underestimated her Ma's reaction to learning about Joe's early release and appearance at the cemetery.

Stella erupted, shaking her head and muttering, throwing words around over the injustice of it all. 'And that poor dead Alice. No one in their right mind believes it was an accident,' she scoffed.

Tilly considered keeping silent about her nasty experience but people needed to be warned about the return of Bingun's notoriously shady local offender. Not only a lousy driver but handy with his fists. On women. But wise enough not to ball his hands and challenge men. Proving he was just a coward.

Cautiously, she shared only the barest details of her encounter with Joe, playing down the severity of her danger.

Of course, Stella launched into another verbal

outburst. 'He threatened you with a loaded rifle? You should report it!'

Tilly sighed. 'Won't help or change anything.'

'The police should be told. You need to call Sergeant John right now.'

'I'm sure he already knows.'

'Did he say he would shoot?'

'Ma, he had a rifle. It was hardly necessary,' Tilly said wryly. 'I got the message. He danced around it. Hot air mostly. Throwing his weight around as usual. I'm sure his trigger finger was itchy until a drifter interrupted.' She explained about her saviour at the cemetery.

'A stranger?' Stella queried, setting out place-mats and cutlery on the table ready for dinner. Anyone unfamiliar in the district was always a topic for discussion.

'I guess so,' Tilly finished chopping, tossed the vegetables into the steamer and stared into space, 'but the way he and Joe exchanged black looks, you'd swear they knew each other. There was something familiar about him. Can't work out what. He had a swag and is obviously just passing through. Yet he seemed a decent enough bloke underneath the thick beard and scruffy appearance. To be honest, I'm not convinced Joe intended to hurt me. Just sprayed me with his usual lashing words. All the same, he's trouble for sure. Since the drifter may have saved my life, I suggested he could camp down by the creek.'

Stella shrugged and poured her small nightly sherry. 'Well, instinct is a fine thing, dear. Sounds like he won't bother us or anyone else while he's around. Probably be gone by morning but if I see that Joe on the street, I'm crossing to the other side. And if you don't go to see Sergeant John first thing in the morning, I will,' she warned.

'All right,' Tilly agreed for the sake of peace more then necessity. 'Probably wise to let him know Joe's up to his usual behaviour already. You'd think he would have been psychologically assessed and given counselling inside.'

Stella shook her head and mumbled, 'Man's too far gone for that. He's the product of a hard upbringing. Old man Hunter was just as mean. Far as I know though, old Harry was never convicted of breaking the law but Joe's a whole other story. It's a sad case. If he wasn't so heartless, a person might even be tempted to feel some sympathy for him.' She sighed heavily. 'Why Alice ever married him I'll never know.'

Later, as she and her mother ate dinner, Tilly deliberated over the Hunter family and how close she had come to being a member. Then she speculated over the mysterious traveller, feeling niggled by a burning curiosity and why she wondered if there was more to him.

Was he hiding something?

2

After an unsettled night's sleep, next morning before school Tilly strode her usual track from the back door along the worn path to the chook yard beyond the farmhouse fence to feed their poultry and gather eggs, Isla alternately disappearing to explore and then returning to hover companionably around her booted heels. An occasional lone kangaroo was out roaming and grazing early, cockatoos and pink galahs scavenging in the grass.

Because she couldn't resist, on her way back to the house she let her gaze stray toward the creek and the stranger's smoking campfire, a small tent pitched nearby. Again, she wondered about him.

Back at the house over breakfast, Stella enjoyed her usual cook up, this morning scrambled eggs. As Tilly filled a bowl with cereal, a spoonful of last season's stewed peaches and yoghurt, she asked her mother, 'What are you your plans today?'

Ma eyed her strangely. 'Get the seedlings in town for the summer vegetable crops.'

'Of course. Sorry.' Her mother had mentioned it last night.

'The tomatoes are thriving in the greenhouse but it's a mite early to set them in the ground.'

Tilly's mind still tended to wander elsewhere. She best get her brain under control before she walked into her classroom. 'Well, don't overdo it.

If you wait until the weekend,' she hinted, 'I can help.'

Fiercely independent, Stella didn't respond, just quietly sipped her second cup of tea.

'Don't forget to take your mobile phone, will you?'

Tilly cringed even as she said it, knowing she was a nag, but driven by deep concern for the little things that she noticed were changing recently for her mother. She waited for her response, knowing that to Stella well-meant genuine consideration was often mistaken for criticism or a personal slight.

'No,' she muttered.

'Good, because when I'm out and about on the farm I always carry mine, too.' Tilly tempered her reminder with a smile of amusement that her daily prompt had been more readily received this morning. 'It's a safety precaution for both of us.'

Stella just grunted. With spring underway and the approach of summer, Tilly was always thankful their glut of fruit and vegies happened in school holidays so she could help her Ma manage all the picking, preserving and jam.

Later, keeping an eye on the clock so she arrived in town soon after eight, Tilly left her mother watching some morning television news before she headed outdoors. She walked to her car saying final goodbyes and showering Isla with lots of affection to last her for the day until she returned this afternoon.

Some sneaky kind of magnetism made her turn to look off into the distance yet again toward the small tent and trail of campfire smoke.

Fire restrictions weren't in force yet but she would keep an eye on the drifter's camp. Go check it out tonight after school by which time he would be long gone.

Leaving the farm, Tilly turned her vehicle right toward Bingun, scooting along the thin strip of Swamp Road so narrow it didn't even rate a centre white line. She was always grateful it was only a five minute drive from the farm along the feeder road until she reached the main road, and another five minutes into town.

Driving past the Hunter place, deserted and neglected now, always proved a challenge because it was the scene of the tragedies that had so deeply affected them all five years ago. With Joe out of prison, wildfire gossip would soon spread around town. The knowledge might be cause for unpleasant reflection on most who knew him and weigh heavily on the fearful few who really had no personal cause for alarm. Although she was sure a handful hoarded nothing but hatred.

For Tilly, his reappearance meant a prudent vigilance and the burden of unwanted additional memories.

On her way into town, massive wind farm turbine blades revolved at the whim of the prevailing westerlies, a vast city of white columns rearing up out of the surrounding flat landscape reminding locals they were in the twenty first century.

Soon Tilly's car rumbled over the new widened concrete bridge crossing Reedy Creek that sluggishly twisted its way through the countryside and into the overflow lagoon from the small town lake.

Bingun was one of those small sleepy country towns still enduring to support its community. Not on a main highway to anywhere but at least the daily bus service connected residents to larger towns and cities. Only lengthy goods trains thundered through its tiny historic station now, mostly bearing mixed freight containers but would soon pause to stop and be filled from the grain bunkers during the coming summer harvest.

A few cars were already angle parked into the kerb along the main street. The old stained glass double doors of Irma's gift shop and cafe were already flung wide, the post office newsagency serving a dual purpose. The double storey Railway Hotel on the corner with its ornate lacy verandas all round was the town's icon still feeding the locals, some upstairs rooms renovated for infrequent passing travellers. Other town business essentials still surviving were the vital IGA, the new medical centre and chemist, a hairdresser, bakery and the garage. There wasn't anything mechanical Neville Reed couldn't make or fix.

Loaded with guilt, Tilly bypassed the police station and backed off reporting the cemetery incident. With Joe Hunter there was always suspicion and consequences. If she dobbed him in, there would be revenge. So she would be damned if she reported him and damned if she didn't. Ma could be in danger, too. She didn't like leaving her alone on the farm all day. At least Isla would bark her head off if she sensed trouble.

Until they knew how his reappearance played

18

out, she kept the knowledge to herself. Only other witness was the drifter and he would probably be gone tomorrow.

Tilly cruised through town to the other end of the single main street and her destination, Bingun Primary School, with about one hundred children in the big old rooms of its historic main red brick building. Not having any siblings, she grew up always wishing for more playmates.

But, Monday to Friday, her teaching gig was bittersweet, on the one hand loving children and enjoying being with them but being reminded daily that they all belonged to someone else. Living with the truth of how much and how deeply she missed the loss of her daughter Anna May and exactly what it meant.

As Tilly locked her car in the small school carpark and strode across the yard, some children yelled out *Good morning, Miss Schroder.* Knowing them all, she responded by name with a smile.

For the most part, Tilly's day passed uneventfully in her Year 6 classroom. But lately she had noticed one of her top students, Chloe Bennett, distracted and anxious. Usually a quiet pleasant pre-teen, lately she lacked concentration, not as focused toward the end of the school term before spring holidays as she normally might be.

So after school Tilly quietly called her aside, waiting until all the other students left the classroom before she asked, 'Everything okay, Chloe?'

The girl's response was a non-committal shrug leaving Tilly concerned. She was usually more bubbly and forthcoming so she smiled and encouraged, 'Nothing worrying you at the moment?'

'Not really,' she said without enthusiasm.

Unconvinced, Tilly could only add quietly, 'Well, if something's troubling you about school and you need to talk, you know I'm always here. Or our school counsellor.'

Chloe looked fearful as though the idea was out of the question but gave a half-hearted nod, clearly either covering something or too afraid to say. Tilly decided if Chloe's abnormal behaviour continued she would be obliged to do mandatory reporting to the Principal, Mrs. Hughes.

The girl seemed definitely troubled and had lost her usual spirit. Maybe it was the thought of the next big step in her education when she moved from the familiar primary school she had known for the past seven years up to a much bigger secondary school in the neighbouring country city of Horsham. Tilly knew she had already been enrolled in the Lutheran College there which would be all new and different. But Chloe was an intelligent if reserved young woman and would adjust, Tilly was sure. At least, she hoped so. Meanwhile she would keep a close eye on the girl.

But just to be sure, Tilly decided to approach Chloe's mum after school. At lunch time she checked the canteen to confirm Karen Bennett was rostered on today. Every Wednesday while in town she did her weekly shopping.

While she was on yard duty, Tilly waited for a chance to approach her. 'Hi, Karen. Would you have time for a chat after school?'

'Hey, Tilly. Sure.'

'Thanks. See you later.'

After school while Tilly waited, Karen bundled Chloe and her two younger sons, Callum and Oliver, into their four wheel drive and asked them to wait.

Returning to speak with Tilly, she checked her watch and said, 'I need to get my groceries home. I have cold stuff in chiller bags.'

'Sure. This won't take a moment.' Tilly launched straight into her concerns. 'Chloe seems distracted in class lately.'

'Oh that seems to happen this time of year,' Karen waved an arm and lightly brushed aside Tilly's observation.

'Really?' she said casually. 'Can I ask why?'

'Oh, you know, we drive right by the Hunter place. She was really affected by that tragedy five years ago. It really bothered her.' Karen frowned in reflection. 'It's about that time of year again.'

Tilly felt confronted by her information, not believing there could be any connection. It seemed that dreadful day had disturbed people more widely than you might think. She would stay vigilant on the girl's behalf.

'Yes, it really was an unfortunate accident.' At least that was the claim and legal verdict at the time. 'Has Chloe ever confided the reason why it upsets her?'

'Not really,' Karen shrugged, casting a glance in the direction of her vehicle where her two younger boys were clearly growing noisy and restless, making their mother anxious to leave. 'I thought she might grow out of it but she does

21

seem more moody this year.'

Tilly dared to tactfully suggest, 'Maybe there's something more behind it that affects her so deeply. I raised the subject today but she said she was okay. I hope you don't mind?'

'No. I'm sure Chloe will be fine.'

Tilly always made sure she was super careful with words when chatting to parents. 'If you haven't tried it, maybe she would be willing to talk to the school counsellor. Or someone privately.'

Karen seemed jolted by the suggestion, that it should be necessary. 'Maybe. I'll see if it passes like other years.'

'Well, let me know if I can help in any way,' Tilly said lightly. 'Chloe really seems very miserable at the moment, doesn't she?'

Karen began moving away but hesitated and turned back. 'He should be released from prison soon.'

Tilly was confounded and challenged by the remark. She, as much as anyone else, knew exactly who she meant. 'Haven't you heard? He's already out!'

'Really? Well, I guess he's done his time. Everyone makes mistakes.' Karen shrugged, waved and left.

When you were personally scarred for life by a tragedy, Tilly knew she would never be able to so easily forgive nor forget.

She certainly wasn't looking forward to seeing Joe Hunter around Bingun again. Even now, she was still haunted by nightmare visions of his sneering demented face through the glare of headlights as his vehicle had ploughed into them.

For now, she didn't believe the chilling memories would ever leave her in peace. As if she hadn't lost and suffered enough already. Tilly shuddered to think Joe Hunter had almost been her father in law.

But like everything else she had done in her life in recent years, she would take one day at a time and when she faced the town's ex-con again, she would do so with the stiff-backed courage she had earned the hard way.

3

On the drive home from school, Tilly mulled over why Chloe Bennett suffered such anxiety around the time of the anniversary of the tragedies that had hit the small community of Bingun hard five years before. Apart from being part of a resident district family, what was the child's connection to them?

After collecting the mail at the gate, being met by an excited Isla and pulling up at the farmhouse, Tilly gathered her school folders from the car boot and went inside. Being close to end of term, she had some subject marking to do later.

When Tilly saw the hump beneath a tea towel on the kitchen bench she only hoped it meant her mother had also taken the time to eat lunch while she was indoors. Without lifting the cloth, she knew from the aroma Ma's efforts were freshly baked scones because Stella always kept them warm that way.

She dumped her school folders on the desk in her room and sauntered back outside to see if her Ma was up for a late afternoon tea. Odds were high she had only grabbed a snack for lunch or forgotten to eat altogether.

At first, Tilly did her usual quick scan for her mother. Nothing. Not entirely unusual. She might be kneeling along the rows. So her daughter looked harder. An urge of anxiety always kicked into play when this happened. Tilly focused and noticed legs and gumboots sticking out the other side of the wheelbarrow. She raced to her side.

'Ma!' Tilly found her sitting on the ground propped up against the cart between the shaft and handles. As she knelt by her side, she aimed for humour and calm in her voice. 'Not like you to take a break.' Her mother's eyes were open but glazed and she looked straight ahead, staring as if confused. 'What have you done to yourself?'

Stella's full length apron over her gardening cargos still bulged, all the pockets stuffed with seed packets, tools and a pair of tough outdoor gloves so something must have happened while she worked.

When her mother's gaze finally cleared, she fixed a glance at her daughter. 'I must have tripped.'

Tilly doubted it. Her mother was still agile and sure footed, although slower in recent times so she had to wonder if it wasn't more or that Ma was covering up. 'Are you hurt anywhere? In pain?'

Stella shook her head. 'I don't think so. Only my pride.'

Her confusion seemed to have subsided. 'How long have you been here?'

Her mother shrugged slightly. 'A while.'

'You didn't think to use your phone?' Tilly bit back the words the moment they escaped. The wrong thing to say right now.

Her mother didn't respond with a familiar retort, apparently still vague to some extent so Tilly believed maybe she had fainted or blacked out. The early September weather wasn't hot yet.

25

Summer was still months away. More than likely Stella had been overdoing it trying to get her first spring plantings into the ground.

Tilly placed her hands beneath her mother's arms. 'Can you help me to get you up?'

Stella made a limp effort but failed to move. 'I don't seem to have the strength, dear.'

'Well you've had a shock but I can't lift you by myself.'

Tilly's mind raced with possibilities. She couldn't drag her mother across to the veranda. Too far and too harsh on the ground even though she wore tough gardening trousers. Clutching at straws before phoning for an ambulance, she stood up and scanned the eastern horizon. Damn if the drifter's tent wasn't still pitched down at the creek. She chewed her lip. Should she?

'Do you have your mobile phone in your apron pocket?' Stella merely frowned, seemingly muddled again. Tilly bent to fish it out and put it in her mother's hand. 'I'm going to see if the stranger down by the creek can help. If you start feeling worse, call me, okay?' She raised a hand and spread her fingers. 'I'll be five minutes.'

Although her mother nodded, Tilly anguished over the thought of leaving her alone but plan B would be quicker than the ambulance which would have to come from Horsham. Half an hour away.

'Isla.' She whistled to the dog, fossicking around the edges of the veggie garden. Her beautiful girl immediately trotted to her side. 'Now you watch out for Ma, okay?' The animal tilted her head as if listening. 'Sit, Isla. Stay with Ma.' The animal sat on her haunches, wagged her tail and remained.

26

Tilly didn't waste time and sprinted around the house to her car, jumped in, fired it up and sped away across the home paddock, ignoring the annoying beeper alarm because she hadn't fastened her seat belt. Within a minute she reached the stranger's campsite. She flung herself from the car and bent to squeeze herself between the fence wires that separated the paddock from Crown land around the creek.

She knew she was overdoing the panic because it seemed that her mother probably just had a nasty fall so she pulled herself to a stop and took a few deep breaths. But she had lost too many people she loved in recent years and she wasn't taking any chances.

As she hesitated, the hatless stranger rose from sitting on a log by his campfire and strode to meet her. As he approached, his long and shaggy dark blonde hair drifting across his forehead, Tilly experienced that weird feeling again that she somehow knew this guy. But with her mind consumed by worry, she pushed all other distracting thoughts to the back of her mind.

She gabbled out an explanation, something like, 'Ma's had a fall, there's no blood but she seems stunned and I can't lift her by myself.'

Even as she pointed toward the farmhouse, he grabbed his hat and within seconds was in the passenger seat alongside her in the car speeding as fast as the rough paddock would allow, his strong silent presence a steadying influence.

She had help. With only the two women living in the farmhouse, Tilly was sometimes gripped by an uneasy yearning for another person for

27

exactly times like these.

Tilly leapt from the car and led the man close at her heels directly around to the north side of the house where her mother still sat, conscious, Isla at her side.

'Good girl.' Tilly crooned to the dog, ruffling her head and ears.

Giving the impression of knowing exactly what he was doing, the man knelt at her mother's side, his deep mellow voice comforting as he carefully pressed her limbs, asking each time if they hurt.

Stella's focus seemed to suddenly sharpen at the sight of him and she actually managed to stammer out, 'No,' to all his queries reassuring Tilly that her Ma didn't appear to have any major injuries. Still, she intended to get her checked out.

Working together, the stranger made short work of placing his strong arms under Stella's body while Tilly lifted her feet. They shuffled across the garden to the veranda, up the broad steps, through the kitchen and set her mother down on the sofa in the sitting area at the far end of their living room.

While the stranger hovered, Tilly brought her Ma a glass of water and felt her forehead, hoping that her pride and maybe some unwanted stiffness or bruises might be the only issues that appeared in the coming days.

'We should call the ambulance. Just to be sure.'

Stella held up a hand, furiously shaking her head. 'Don't fuss. I'll be fine.'

'I'll make an appointment in the morning with Doctor Singh at the medical centre — '

'You. Will. Not!'

Tilly's gaze doubled in disbelief at her mother's fierce objection. 'All right,' she said softly to pacify the agitation. 'I'll get you a cuppa but you're to stay put on that sofa.' She pointed a finger and smiled.

Appeased by her daughter's agreement, Stella relaxed. Tilly turned her attention to the stranger, standing astride, his big capable hands on his hips but for all his muscular strength, looking lost.

'We're much obliged to you. And I'm sorry about all the hand waving and gabbling down there.' Tilly felt hot with embarrassment that she had lost control earlier but Ma was all she had.

Behind the jungle of beard that almost covered his neck as well, his mouth twitched as though grinning. 'Happy to help.'

Lost for anything else to do right at that moment, Tilly extended a hand. 'Tilly Schroder and my mum, Stella.'

He accepted her hand and nodded. The touch was warm and rough with a bone crushing grip. A countryman's handshake. Impossible not to notice that he didn't introduce himself in return.

Stella's forehead wrinkled into a frown and she exchanged a casual glance with her daughter before she closely eyed their mysterious Good Samaritan.

'Thank you for your help,' she said weakly. He nodded. After an awkward moment of silence and with more energy, she probed, 'You from around here?'

Tilly admired her mother's courage in asking such a blunt question and was encouraged by the fact that her mind seemed sharper now than when she had been first found.

There was a long enough pause before the stranger responded during which a cloud of tension settled over the room, intuition reinforcing Tilly's hunch that there was much more to this stranger than either of them could possibly know.

He shuffled and murmured, 'Once.'

Tilly's eyebrows shot up with interest. She knew it!

But Stella didn't seem at all surprised. 'Thought you looked familiar.'

Tilly's radar locked onto the subject of their joint attention. Frowning, she concentrated and squinted to focus on him until a niggle of possibility formed in the back of her mind. It couldn't be. Could it? Well, why not? The return of the prodigal son.

Tilly glanced across at her mother who raised her eyebrows as if to say *Are you thinking what I'm thinking?*

Tilly turned to their helper. Squinting to see beyond the hair hanging across his forehead, she met his clear blue eyes with a direct challenging gaze. She hadn't noticed *how* blue because although he had approached her at the cemetery, he had kept his distance. Besides, his eyes were in the shadow of the battered hat that had seen plenty of wear and better days, his hair was long and his face hidden behind a substantial beard. Perhaps an image for anonymity he deliberately chose to foster. Especially if returning home and he didn't want to be recognised.

Not uncommon that he was nothing like his brother. Christian, who was more like his parents, Joe and Alice, with a darker complexion and those dusky flashing eyes he had only ever turned in Tilly's direction. This person was the blonde haired blue-eyed charmer and younger son who never seemed to fit in.

Feeling foolish for not recognising him sooner, in a catch of breath and with half a smile Tilly managed to say, 'It *is* you.'

How could this kind and masculine man be the same gorgeous but irresponsible womaniser she remembered? Rude to stare, even at someone she had known all her life apart from the last few years and should have identified, but she couldn't help it. With decent clothes and a shave, he might come close to looking how he used to be.

She had been thrown by the maturity, no doubt learned from life's lessons these past years, and the lean and tanned, haunted individual that replaced the sandy haired carefree beach boy in her class, a girl magnet all through high school.

Stella sat up straighter and shook her head. 'Well I'll be damned. Lucas Hunter.'

Not a coincidence. They both knew the reason he was back.

'Why are you hiding your identity?' her mother asked.

Luke found his voice and explained, turning slightly so he kept both women in his line of sight to address them. 'To keep a low profile now Joe's been released. I figured with nowhere else to go he'd head home to the farm. It's neglected and no longer a working proposition, at least for

31

him, but I'm thinking he'll stick around as long as possible. Just want to keep an eye on him. Make sure he doesn't step out of line again.'

Stella scoffed and muttered, 'I know he's your father Lucas but Joe Hunter never cared what he said or did to anyone, especially your mother,' she muttered darkly, 'and he certainly never bothered about being on the wrong side of the law. You won't change him.'

Luke clenched his jaw, accepting her sharp truth. 'Understand that. Just want to make sure no one else comes to any harm.'

'That will be a job for the police, Lucas. Not your responsibility,' Stella cautioned. 'I'm thinking that since Tilly explained what happened at the cemetery it would be safer for your health to step back and stay out of it.'

Tilly crossed and rubbed her arms, still astonished that the man in their kitchen was Christian's brother. 'Where have you been all these years?'

His gaze settled on her with a gentle warmth but a bleakness edged his voice. 'Wandering. Restless. Getting work where I can.' His shrug was casual but it was clear this man was still living with the nightmare, too. 'I've been back every year around this time.' He looked directly at Tilly. 'To make sure you were okay. This is the first time I've been sprung.' His tone softened. 'In a good cause.'

He covered her with a heartbreaking gaze of such compassion Tilly almost burst into tears. She swallowed hard. 'I'm doing fine.' A lie and his forgiving glance told her he knew it. A conversation for another time.

'Thank you for what you did yesterday. I sensed you and Joe knew each other but rejected the idea out of hand because it was so crazy. God,' Tilly slapped a hand to her forehead, feeling hot with embarrassment, 'you probably intended camping by the creek anyway.'

His stance was more relaxed now, his tension eased. 'I usually head bush to stay hidden.' He turned to her mother. 'Good to see you again, Mrs. Schroder.'

She waved an arm. 'Call me Stella.' She paused before adding, 'We used to be neighbours, Lucas. You didn't feel you could trust us enough to come and pay your respects?'

Luke shook his head. 'To be honest, Stella, being a member of the notorious Hunter family, I felt too ashamed. Wasn't sure how I would be received.'

'You might look more approachable if you shaved off that beard,' Stella muttered, 'but you certainly weren't responsible for anything that happened five years ago. We can't choose our parents and we must all make our own lives.' She eyed him fondly. 'You favour your mother and for that you should be grateful. She was a fine woman and loyal to a man who didn't deserve it.' Almost immediately she changed topic. 'Dinner's not ready yet but you're welcome to join us. Repay you for saving Tilly and helping me into the house. You look like you might appreciate a shower.'

'Obliged to you. No trouble?'

Stella scoffed. 'Course not. Bathroom's in the same place. Hasn't moved in the past five years,' she chuckled. 'Everything you need's in there.

33

Since I'm not allowed to move,' she complained, pointedly glaring at her daughter, 'Tilly will get you a fresh towel.'

Still stunned, she mumbled, 'Of course.'

Tilly hadn't seen Luke since the night of the accident. Apparently, he had disappeared immediately after the funeral, the Hunter farm deserted ever since. Of course, if life had gone according to plan, he would have been her brother in law by now, his parents Joe and Alice her in laws, she would have been married in the sturdy bluestone church of St. Peters in town with a wedding ring on her finger and she would be sending her daughter, Anna May, off to school next year.

Seeing Luke after all this time, she grew overwhelmed afresh by the impact of all the love and plans and dreams that could have been but would never be, stamped out by a careless drunk on that unforgettable dark and rainy spring night. Joe Hunter. Luke and Christian's father. A night when so many lives were affected and changed in the flash of headlights and a sickening crunch.

With Luke's reappearance and forced to remember that night, deep in her heart Tilly knew she still felt confusion and regret over what happened. If he hadn't been drunk.

If he hadn't been lying on the back seat.

If he had been driving his own car instead of his responsible older brother. Christian, at the wheel.

As Luke moved across the room heading for the hallway, Stella snapped, 'Tilly, Luke will need that towel.'

Stella's voice punctured her compelling

thoughts and drew her back to the moment. 'Yes, Ma, I heard,' she said sharply, annoyed at her lapse of attention and being bawled out by her mother. She followed Luke down the hall toward the linen cupboard.

He half turned back to her, his expression guarded, where it had been open with her mother. 'Thanks, Tilly. Don't mean to be a bother.'

'You mean no more than you used to be?' she quipped, then, seeing the cringe of hurt cross his face immediately wished her tactless jibe could be taken back.

Steady and quiet, holding her gaze as she placed the towel into his arms, Luke said, 'I'm not the same person I used to be.'

Tilly could see that the sandy-haired local heart-throb had grown up and a remorseful wary man had taken his place. Just the same as the smitten carefree very pregnant woman very much in love with the oldest Hunter son had her own world shattered that same night, too, and likewise had grown up fast. They all still bore scars and regrets. Probably be a part of all their lives forever.

'Five years have changed us all,' she murmured. 'I'll see if I can find some of Dad's old clothes. If you leave yours on the laundry floor I'll toss them into the wash tonight and leave them at your camp tomorrow when they're dry.'

Back in the kitchen, Tilly busied herself by brewing her Ma the promised cup of tea and gratefully eyed the scones. A big pot of spicy pumpkin soup should do it. Maybe toss in a handful of fresh garden herbs and pasta to add more substance to their meal.

Tilly was neither interested nor encouraged any potential boyfriends or lovers. Even though she was closing in on thirty and it was five long years since she had been briefly engaged, men didn't figure on her radar with any level of importance.

Now and again she might be hit with need or loneliness but she was mostly rewarded by her job and content in her life with Ma. One school week tumbled into another. Terms, semesters and seasons passed with familiar rhythm, all blending together until she dealt with one year before facing the next.

While dinner simmered on the stove and before Luke reappeared, she went through the laundry to grab more logs for the fire and fish out a few bottles of her favourite Cascade Light lager from the second refrigerator.

Back in the kitchen, a recovering Stella sat up with a tinge of pink on her cheeks and Luke had reappeared. She dropped, rather than placed, the logs in the fireside basket, straightened and stared.

Her father's old jeans were a neat fit and length, the checked shirt sleeves rolled to the elbows. His washed pale hair was darker, hanging longer, almost touching the base of his neck. Still that same tilted smile though more restrained and, she suspected, less likely to appear these days. And where once his handsome face and skin, what she could see of it, glowed golden from the sun now it was lean and brown, his body more muscled from outdoor work.

While she stood speechless, Luke said quietly,

'I left my clothes in the laundry.'

'Thanks. I'll . . . um . . . put them in the machine.'

'Took the liberty. Already did.'

Caught by surprise, Tilly faltered. 'Oh. Great.' Clearly a man used to taking care of himself.

When she offered him a beer it was declined. 'Don't touch the stuff anymore. Thanks, anyway.'

Was his rejection a consequence of that fateful night? 'Sure.' She replaced one bottle in the fridge, hesitant to drink in front of him. But he seemed man enough to take it so she snapped off the lid and poured herself a glass.

Instead, she grew irritated to feel any softness for Luke when thoughts of irresponsibility and fault still lingered in her mind. Yet she struggled against the fact that he seemed different now and had probably saved her life yesterday or, at the least, rescued her from a knotty situation. Grappling with her push and pull emotional dilemma, she turned her back and vigorously stirred the soup before setting the table and dishing it up in huge earthenware bowls.

'Am I allowed to move now?' Stella quipped, swinging her feet over the side of the sofa.

Tilly smiled. 'Can you make it on your own?'

She forgot sometimes but knew better than to fuss. All the same, she eyed her mother carefully as she moved. She *seemed* okay. A hard working compassionate woman with a strong mind of her own who resisted being told what to do. The rock and saviour who had pulled her through the turmoil of five years ago, while also dealing by stoic acceptance with the sudden loss of her husband two years later.

In contrast, Tilly had been devastated by her father's untimely death. Her parents' offsider in every way. Ever the teacher, Ma had led by example to remember her loved one well but move on.

Reflecting, Tilly felt frustrated that she moved mechanically through every day. With Luke and Joe Hunter back in Bingun, maybe the universe was sending a signal and this was the catalyst that might finally propel her toward discovering what really happened back then. For she was convinced more information still lurked hidden and she was determined, somehow, to expose it.

With the survivors from five years ago together again for the first time, could she finally break free and relegate the tragedies to the past?

When Tilly returned to the moment from her mental wandering, she found her soup half eaten and Luke idly chatting to her mother. Eyeing the older woman, shoulders rounded in her familiar weariness, Tilly decided, come tomorrow, she would be driving Ma into town to get checked out at the Medical Centre. Instinct usually served her well. All was not right for this tough country lady who was only a few years short of her seventieth birthday.

Dinner passed comfortably enough with safe conversation, avoiding both issues on all their minds at the moment. It was taking time for Tilly to adjust to this hairy neighbour returning to their midst again. To reconcile this reserved stranger with the loud social livewire who had so suddenly left.

Her long held resentment was being challenged because Luke had certainly changed. He *seemed* genuine and Tilly was not indifferent to the fact that he had also lost two family members at the time. His brother Christian, of course, but also his mother, Alice, some weeks prior in another sudden devastating and baffling accident.

Her death was supposedly the reason for Joe's drunken inattention that night which Tilly refused to believe. At the notorious intersection. Christian barely had time to react, had just jammed on the brakes with hardly a chance to glance sideways. But predicting the magnitude of the oncoming impact, staring straight past Christian and out the driver's side window, Tilly had seen it all, instinctively folded her hands across her stomach and screamed.

Deep in thought, Tilly's focus only revived again when Luke rose and thanked them for the meal. Stirring herself, she cleared the table while Stella slowly retired to her favourite living room recliner.

Without being asked and darting her some cautious sideways looks, Luke worked silently alongside Tilly at the sink, rinsing plates and cutlery while she stacked the dishwasher. A cautious distance remained between them and she felt no desire to talk.

She couldn't help reflecting how different the present day Luke was to the one she knew growing up. The boy and teenager had been careless more than carefree, a young man who pushed boundaries. Everyone knew the Hunter household wasn't a happy one. How could it be when ruled by their tyrant father, Joe, who beat up his wife and whipped his sons?

It was obvious back then that, for the youngest Hunter son, disappearing had been his way of escaping a tough family life.

Yet his older brother, Christian, also possessing the wild Hunter streak had seemed to cope, or at least separate his family and farm working life from socialising among their close district youth group.

From habit, Tilly set the kettle boiling. Out of courtesy, she felt obliged to ask. 'Will you stay for a cuppa?'

Luke's hesitation was revealing. Tilly sensed his reluctance since she had hardly been the most gracious host tonight but as Ma always said *Manners cost us nothing*.

'Sure. Thanks.' Once again he pushed a hand into the hair that kept falling across his forehead without the hat to keep it in place.

To anyone who didn't know him he would look threatening and scruffy. 'You should get the whole lot chopped off. Hair and beard,' she chided, pouring the teas and handing them around. 'Josie's salon is still open. Go pay her a visit. She could do with the custom. Times in the country are hard.'

His blue eyes glinted with deliberation. 'I might just do that. With the summer harvest coming up, I'll be looking for work. Guess the least I can do is look respectable.' Backed up against the kitchen counter, drinking his tea and looking ready to run, he glanced across at her.

Tilly knew Luke Hunter would bear his

family's stigma when he had done nothing wrong himself, grudgingly acknowledging he was a brave man to return and face everyone. She was still deep down angry that his father Joe was only punished for a few years on a decision of *death by misadventure* then allowed to go on and live his life again when her fiancé and baby never had that chance.

It would be interesting to see the reaction of locals when old Joe walked down the main street of Bingun as though nothing had happened.

Above her thoughts, Luke said, 'Since I don't have any fixed address, I might head into the police station tomorrow and let them know I'm around.'

'See Josie first,' Tilly teased.

She brooded over how Joe Hunter's reappearance in town would affect everyone's lives. The first person who came to mind was Chloe Bennett. She would keep a close eye on the girl at school.

It seemed like Luke intended to keep tabs on his father and the family farm although she imagined it was deep in debt. Since it wasn't a working property, it would be worth less than its potential value and difficult to rejuvenate as a going concern. Since Luke had just admitted he was looking for work off-farm, he certainly didn't intend being a part of that process.

Luke's cup rattled back into its saucer. 'I'll be off now. Thank you for your kindness ladies.'

'You're welcome,' Stella said faintly, sounding weary.

'Goodnight.' Torn with conflicting emotions,

Tilly didn't show him to the door. Just stared at him, frowning, and rubbed her arms.

With a nod, he slapped his hat onto his head and disappeared out onto the veranda. Before he strode away into the night back to his campsite on the creek, she watched through the screen door as he paused to give Isla some attention and a few kind murmured words, heartened by the friendly gesture to her cherished animal.

The father's physical abuses didn't seem to have trickled down to the next generation, then. Reassuring. Joe Hunter was well known for kicking his dogs.

4

Next morning, aiming to keep the visit brief, Tilly detoured to Luke's creekside camp to drop off his laundered clothes before she drove into town for another school day.

As she pulled up, he sat on a tree stump before his campfire, a thin trail of smoke lazily climbing into the calm morning air, his hands cupped around a tin mug.

For a wildly envious moment, the tranquil scene pulled her thoughts toward ditching school for the day to join him. She couldn't recall when she had last made time to just *be* like that.

Luke caught her gaze through the windscreen and she saw hope flare across his face. He rose, easily striding to meet her. Feeling embarrassed, she knew he had probably watched her progress since leaving the farmhouse.

Tilly climbed from the car, retrieved his clothes from the back seat and handed them over.

'Thanks. I appreciate this.'

'I guess you don't get much help on the road.'

Tilly despised herself for feeling agro this early in the day. Leftover from the earlier strong words with her mother? Clearly Luke Hunter was not what she once knew him to be.

His bushy eyebrows twitched. 'You'd be surprised.'

Tilly faltered at the glimpse of playfulness she

remembered. Everything else about the man had changed.

They floundered in the uncomfortable silence that fell between them. Luke's eyes, as blue as the Wimmera sky, almost begged her with appeal. Seeking forgiveness? Acceptance? For Tilly it was too early in the day to address the past.

'I know you must hate me,' he murmured.

An assumption. Close to the truth but not quite. 'Why would I do that?'

He swallowed and shuffled. For a grown man he looked mighty awkward. 'Because I was drunk that night. I should have been driving.'

'Yes you should and, for that, I pitied you. That Christian coped and was stronger, that you turned to drink. I know your home situation was destructive but I never hated you, Luke. At the time, I was too busy recovering after the accident. Grieving for a baby I would never hold in my arms and the loss of the man I expected to spend the rest of my life with.' When Luke seemed about to speak again, Tilly held up a hand. 'I don't have time for this now. I need to get to school.'

'I'd appreciate it if we could talk sometime.'

His gentle plea was so sincere her heart wrenched, knowing they had all suffered in the past and were dealing with the ongoing consequences in their lives. For Tilly, memories were always with her but flooded back more heavily at this time of year. Now there were new complications in the mix. Joe Hunter's return and Christian's irresponsible brother standing in front of her. But as she was already starting to realise, Luke Hunter was

44

now a different person. It was probably uncharitable and hasty to label him based on the past.

After a reasonable night's sleep, at least as good as it got for her these days, and time to think, she still wasn't feeling generous toward Luke Hunter at the moment.

To satisfy him for now, she said, 'Maybe.'

At her crumb of promise, his lined forehead and serious manner eased. 'I'd appreciate it,' he urged. 'Would do us both good.'

How could he know what helped her and what didn't? After another strained pause, Tilly sighed and lifted a shoulder in a careless shrug. 'If you want.' Lighter, she added, 'Tell Josie I sent you.'

Then she turned her back on him, clambered behind the wheel and drove across the paddock to the road heading into town for another school day.

How was she supposed to concentrate with all this shit happening? Joe Hunter out of prison and loose in Bingun again. Luke Hunter back in town imposing a new slant on her painful memories and lingering grievance over that night. Memorable for all the wrong reasons. Well that just topped off both their happy families now, didn't it?

Thinking of family, Tilly had set her mind on making an appointment for today at the Medical Centre to get her Ma checked out. But before she left, Stella almost blew a fuse in the kitchen at the suggestion, so she backed off. She hoped her mother might have mellowed to the idea overnight. She should have known better.

Didn't mean Tilly couldn't make an appointment for herself to see if the doctor had any
more information than Stella was most likely not
sharing.

And halfway into town, Tilly realised she
hadn't even thought to ask Luke if he wanted a
lift into town. It was a long walk. She felt bad
and considered turning around but that would
make her late for school.

★ ★ ★

Luke checked his campfire was out, shouldered
his backpack and strode out to power-walk
across country into Bingun. That way he made
the hike in under an hour. Walking had long
since become his therapeutic friend. Along with
any labouring work he could find, it kept him fit
and helped him sleep.

He hoped Josie's rate for a haircut was less
than the notes in his wallet. He had learned to
survive with cash and a cheap second-hand
outdated mobile that only worked when he was
near civilization and free Wi-Fi.

He had already scouted around the Hunter
farm and been into town to scope it out. That
excursion had drawn some interesting looks.
Only needed to top up some supplies today then
head back to camp. Always his solace wherever
he happened to be.

This side of town, the old red brick water
tower loomed into view first. Main Street was
quiet, a few cars and utes about, and even fewer
people. Two older women further down chatting

in the sun gave him the once-over as he passed on the other side. He paused outside *Josie's Salon* and wondered if she would recognise him. The return of another unwanted Hunter.

When he opened the door, a bell jingled. Three pairs of female eyes snapped in his direction. True, he wasn't a good look but he was here to stay and aimed to change that right now. Whether that stay was long term depended on two things. The attitude of the locals and a woman.

As Josie excused herself from a client and strolled to greet him, her curious gaze raked him over. Frowning, she hadn't figured it out yet. She was still the petite little blonde he remembered. He darted a glance at the occupied ring finger of her left hand. Of course she would be married. She was still a looker but not his type.

'Josie,' he greeted quietly.

Her face lit up with a perky smile. 'Been trying to work you out.'

'Luke.' He removed his hat and combed fingers through his hair, not that it made much difference.

Her gaze doubled. 'Hunter!'

Josie said it so loud the women seated beside each other across the room didn't miss a word. Their heads leaned closer and they whispered. Yep, word was out.

'Well I'll be damned.'

Same words had tumbled out of Stella's mouth. 'As you can see,' he ran a hand over his whiskered face, 'I need your skilled hands. Tilly sent me.'

Josie's hazel eyes rounded and nearly popped.

'You've been out to Schroders?'

Luke was well aware how it looked, the tricky connection and stigma. 'We used to be neighbours,' he said calmly.

'Of course,' she stuttered.

The first of many judgements he'd need to fix. *Patience, Luke,* he told himself. *This is gonna take a while.* 'Do I need to make an appointment?' he prompted as Josie continued to stare.

She dropped her gaze to the open lined book on the counter. 'Not if you're prepared to wait.' She whipped a glance back toward her waiting ladies. 'Twenty minutes?'

Luke guessed it was safer if he stayed put. Less chance of running into locals. Besides, until he found a job and life took on a routine, he had all the time in the world. 'Fine.'

'Take a seat.'

Josie indicated the chairs and a table piled with women's magazines by the window. Not totally inconspicuous but he was content to watch life in Bingun roll by awhile.

After Josie cleaned him up, he'd feel more comfortable about being out in public. As a teenager, he felt like he owned the town, was part of the community, school, and never bothered what folks thought. Nowadays, his natural caution gained over the years kept him guarded. When he left this salon, he'd be pretty much recognisable again and prepared himself for that.

One woman left, pointedly gaping on her way out the door and when the other had a head full of rollers and Josie settled her under a dryer, she returned to Luke.

'Come through.'

It was a rare treat to finally feel more settled, getting his hair cut in a ladies' salon because there was no barber in town, smelling sweet while she washed and massaged his hair. Not until he was seated before a mirror wrapped in a black plastic cape with wet hair to his shoulders did Josie attempt conversation.

'So, you staying in town, Luke?' She grabbed her scissors and began to work.

He remembered she used to be chatty and friendly, and hoped she didn't ask too many questions. 'That's the plan.'

'I see your Dad's back.'

Shit. 'Yep.'

'You living out on the farm?'

'Nope.'

He didn't follow up on that topic, hoping Josie took the hint. It had bugged him for two days so he planned on calling into the police station and reporting the cemetery incident. Maybe not mention the rifle, just the threat. Another pair of eyes on Joe wouldn't hurt.

'So, you looking for work?'

Great chunks of his damp hair fell to the floor, leaving Luke debating whether its disappearance as security in recent years was a wise move after all. The loss was radical, about to uncover the true man again.

'Sure am. Any ideas?'

'Well, the merchant that operates the bunkers outside of town is moving the last of their stored grain before the coming harvest. Heard they're wanting truck drivers.'

49

'Thanks. I'll check it out.' He had an endorsed licence and it suited him fine to be working alone. Less chance of conflict all round while he eased back into Bingun life again. For how long it lasted was still up for grabs. Steering the conversation away from himself and having noticed her rings, Luke asked, 'So you're married now?'

Which released a sermon of information. 'Yes,' Josie glowed, 'to Peter Anderson. Bruce and Wendy's son?'

Luke nodded but stayed silent.

'Before we were twenty-one. But we knew. I always wanted to work in the beauty industry so Elaine gave me an apprenticeship here. Once Pete and I had kids, I did mobile hairdressing for a bit but then Pete built in half of the back veranda for me and we set it up as a salon. Handy for keeping an eye on the children. My elderly neighbours give me a tingle first and then drop in.

'Now our oldest girls Sasha and Lila are at school and kinder, my mother Wendy babysits our toddler, Aidan, when she can or I place him in our local childcare room at the Kindergarten. Works in well with Lila being four and a kindy kid this year. Sasha rides her bike to school. I still take clients at home but I'm mostly in here now.' She beamed. 'I bought the business from Elaine last year. Times in the country can be tough but the locals have been great and supported me.'

As she talked, Josie's hands finished their work. She even clippered off the worst of his beard and gave him a shave back to a shadow. He thought the blow dryer on his hair was a bit much but he gaped at the skilled transformation. Damn if underneath five years of disguise, he was still a half decent bloke.

'What do you think?' she grinned.

'Nice. Thanks.' He grew bashful, pleased with the result. About time he did it for sure. His second thought was what Tilly would think.

At the counter, Josie said, 'You're different now, Luke. In a good way,' she hastily added when he raised eyebrows in amusement.

'You think?'

When he chuckled, the familiarity felt good. So much easier talking to someone he knew. Not holding back with a fellow stranger he'd just met. Making surface conversation. Never going deeper or letting himself get close to another person. Bingun life might suit him after all. But he knew all encounters wouldn't be this encouraging.

He paid Josie and still had some notes left for a few basic supplies from the IGA. Leaving the salon, he headed across the street to the beautiful old brick police station. With every step, he second-guessed his decision and almost turned away but forced his boots forward and went inside. Surely old Sergeant Blake wouldn't still be here, too? That might prove awkward. They'd been on first name terms back when.

He wasn't. Seemed he'd retired down the coast.

Sergeant John Turner wasn't much older than Luke. He introduced himself and explained the reason for his visit. *Sergeant John* as he'd heard Stella refer to him, was on top of the Joe Hunter situation but appreciated the chat to learn more

51

background on a personal level. Although Luke kept his information general and didn't go into detail.

He left the station feeling he'd made a true friend. The first in a long time. After a productive morning in town, his backpack crammed with fresh supplies and putting his name down for work at the grain company office, Luke strode back across country, looking and feeling like a worthy man. By family association, he knew he'd have to prove himself and rebuild people's trust but he was up for the challenge.

He was back where his heart belonged, in more ways than one, and he would fight damn hard to make this potential new life work.

★ ★ ★

Later that afternoon, Tilly motored light-heartedly out of town in her car, driver side window down to inhale the brisk afternoon spring air, the radio on a country music station. She was eager to get home and make sure Stella was still okay. She had already phoned and checked during her lunch break at school, much to her mother's annoyance, which she bore in relief knowing her worst nightmare hadn't come true and Joe hadn't paid an unwelcome visit.

Soon after she turned onto Swamp Road, a ute turned too and followed, trailing close behind. A local should know better. The driver didn't stay put for long but sped up, closed the gap between the vehicles and pulled out to pass.

Muttering to herself about crazy drivers, Tilly

pulled further over to let him drive by. And recognised Joe. Grinning. Immediately he swerved back in front of her, cutting her off so she was forced to brake hard and stop. She was shocked to see him driving. After his conviction and imprisonment, would he still have a licence?

Tilly knew danger when she faced it. He'd been waiting for her. Knew where she would be and what time. Like at the cemetery on the anniversary of those she loved who had so tragically died. And today, returning from school.

She started breathing slow to calm down. If she didn't get out, Joe would come to her car. Seated inside and immobile, she'd be an easy target for whatever he had planned and didn't like her chances. Outwardly she needed to appear in control, even though inside she was a mess.

With anger fuelling her confidence, Tilly determined to front him. That was it. Enough. The reality of her life now Joe was back meant she would be meeting him on the street and threatened if she didn't take a stand. Now. At least in prison he had been out of sight, if not out of mind. Never that.

If she survived this encounter, she would report him and lodge a formal complaint.

Joe Hunter sure knew how to pick his moments. A lonely cemetery. But fate was on her side and that attempt was foiled. A lonely country road. She glanced down at her car clock. The school bus would be along but, with regular drop offs, not for another twenty or thirty minutes.

Tilly braced herself and set a plan in motion because Joe was staggering from his vehicle

53

holding a rifle, waving it around like a golf club as he approached.

She fumbled for her mobile and set it to video then slowly eased herself from the car, staying behind the security of her open door.

'Your driving hasn't improved,' she called out, keeping the phone half hidden within the palm of her hand as she filmed. 'Two personal visits within days? What's the problem?'

As he wandered unsteadily closer, Tilly noted the bleary eyes. Which meant his finger could easily slip on that trigger and go off any time in any direction. He was often drunk by midday. This late in the day meant he was probably seriously pissed, mentally unsound and physically dangerous.

Tilly was under no illusion about the extent of her personal trouble.

'Poleesh paid me a visit.'

'You're surprised? Considering where you've just come from? I'm sure John was just doing his job.'

'Cop mentioned the shemetery.'

She frowned. 'I've been in school all day.'

'You got a phone.'

'And I'm using it now for video evidence.' Tilly wondered if, in his present condition, he even realised what that meant. 'In the unlikely event anything happens to me.'

'I'll destroy it.'

'They'll trace your tyre tread. Your rifle shells. And, according to what you just said, they already know we've *met* at the cemetery.'

Tilly heard a growl from deep in his throat. He

54

staggered a few steps closer. *Oh, please God* . . .

She watched Joe's face twist with anger and soon learned the reason why. 'Another woman fornicator,' he lashed out. 'Being a whore with my son.'

Yes, Tilly admitted, she and Christian had been lovers before marriage. But he said *another woman*. Who was the other one?

And had it been a coincidence that Sergeant John went to see him today or not? The only other person who knew about their cemetery meeting was Luke and her mother. Stella wouldn't be bothered. She was too engrossed in her gardening at the moment. Which just left Luke. Would he inform on his own father? There was certainly no love lost between them.

'Stop living in the past, Joe. Move on. Mind your own business and let us all live our lives.'

He sneered and spat on the ground. 'You take care of Shtella, now.'

The cheek. Using Ma as leverage to keep her quiet? If this rotten excuse for a human being touched a hair on her mother's head —

Tilly looked up and Joe, his sly faculties sharpening, turned at the humming sound of tyres on a gravel road behind him and the approach of a smart four wheel drive coming in from the opposite direction, heading toward the main road. Dave Meyer, Tilly recognised as he pulled up, probably returning to his property on the other side of town.

Blocked by Joe's slewed ute, he emerged from his vehicle.

Tilly closed her eyes and sent up a prayer of

thanks then stopped the video and tossed the phone onto her driver's seat. Joe, she noticed, had quickly hobbled back to his ute and tossed the rifle inside.

'Hey Dave,' Tilly called out. 'Joe's just skidded in gravel. Not used to driving just yet.'

She despised herself for making excuses for the old bugger but while Joe had his back turned to her looking away, focused on Dave, Tilly frowned and shook her head in warning. Dave dipped a brief nod in understanding.

'You okay, Joe?' the town's gentleman bachelor asked in concern, a member of their small Lutheran congregation.

Their local infamous felon muttered something, started up his engine, skidding the rear of his ute so that it swung in gravel as he took off.

As they both looked after his wall of dust, Dave said, 'Heard he was back. Need me to follow you home?'

Tilly grinned to herself. He guessed exactly what had happened but she shook her head.

'Need to report anything, I can be a witness.'

'Thanks. I'll be fine. Aiming to call in on Sergeant John tomorrow.'

Dave smiled, gave half a wave and returned to his vehicle. He was a lovely man. A hard working gentle giant. Still above handsome even past middle age.

Dave drove off, Tilly climbed back into her car and trembling with shock in the wake of a second confrontation, motored the rest of the way slowly home wondering how long her current run of luck would last.

5

An unsettled Tilly turned in at the farm gate to find Isla sitting on her haunches patiently waiting. She opened her door, collected the mail and the dog leapt in. At the house, Tilly turned off the engine and just sat in the car, allowing herself to recover from Joe's second holdup, Isla's head in her lap as she gently stroked her beautiful spoilt animal.

Life had continued quietly ordinary for years but suddenly so much was happening, forcing a transition. It was like the universe was trying to tell her something. She had knowingly buried the tragic past event for far too long, refusing to deal with the repercussions it had wrought in her life. Shoved it so deep to the back of her mind and instead had focused on living rather than addressing the massive change it had meant at the time.

But now, somehow, she needed to dredge up those thoughts from the depths of her subconscious and force herself to find enough courage to open the wounds and face her emotional demons. To seek answers to the questions that those reflections made.

The anger over the one split second that had deprived her of Christian in her life.

The ache for the loss of an unborn baby girl.

The guilt for conceiving the child outside of marriage against the principles of her faith. At the time, Tilly had sensed her parents' disappointment when they announced the unexpected news, but they loved and respected Christian and had stood by the couple.

Once or twice over the years, Tilly had allowed herself to dwell briefly on alternative outcomes. How life might have turned out differently if Christian had survived but not Anna May. Would they have still married? Or would losing their daughter, the catalyst for their engagement back then, have meant they no longer had something to force a commitment or even keep them together?

Would the loss have been too great for them? Would their love have survived? Not all marriages were for a lifetime.

She and Christian had both been adults, considered themselves mature. Those four years while she was away studying at university to be a teacher were heady but emotionally strained. Returning to Bingun for hot weekend sex in the back of the car, in the hayshed, in a paddock in the grass by moonlight.

Their loving had been romantic and steamy and real. From the heart.

They endured until she attained her degree and returned to Bingun to teach, with Christian practically running the Hunter farm, helped by Luke, their father rarely sober, Alice somehow keeping the family together.

She and Christian knew they would eventually marry but until Tilly was out earning a teaching salary, and with both he and Luke only earning meagre wages working for Joe, they chose to wait until they built up enough savings to give them independence.

And what if Anna May had survived but not Christian? Either way, Tilly felt her heart breaking anew. She would have been a single mother raising her child but not alone. Her own parents would have been front and centre, and she would be living in exactly the same place as she did now, in the Schroder farmhouse, surrounded and nourished by the small doting family.

Although she dreaded the thought that Joe would have been her daughter's paternal grandfather and knew his mean nature since childhood, the knowledge could not stop her falling in love with his oldest son. In contrast, Tilly adored Alice Hunter, Christian's mother and Stella's best friend, the close *aunt* in her life who gave her sons twice the love to try and compensate, she guessed, for their abusive father.

Would the devastation of losing Christian but holding their baby girl in her arms have been sufficient blessing and memory in proof of their love? The agony of course being that she would never know.

And of course the ultimate ideal ending; what if they had all survived? Her chest hurt as if her heart was physically aching. Five years later, she trusted they would be happily married with probably another child or children. She fingered the fine plaited rope charm bracelet that never left her wrist, Christian's first gift to her all those years ago.

Her thoughts strayed wider. Would Luke have stayed in Bingun? Even from the small amount of time she had spent in his company since his return, she sensed his genuine regret. They all wished life could have been different. If only . . .

Because his mother had died in a baffling farm accident just weeks before the accident that claimed Christian and tore a lifeless Anna May from her body, Tilly suspected Luke would still have left the district. And with Joe in gaol, why not? His whole family had been split apart.

In the bleakness and hopelessness of it all, of what might have happened against what actually did, tears slid down her cheeks and she let them slowly and steadily fall, quietly sobbing. Isla sensed her sadness and whined, nudging her wet nose into Tilly's hands.

As the torrent gradually eased, she knew dealing with Joe and Luke returning, plus opening up her emotions was just the beginning. She still had a long way to go. Part of that journey was what seemed the impossibility of opening her heart up to another while she still desperately clung to the shreds of her fierce first love.

And there were still two difficult conversations yet to be had today. With a deep sigh and feeling like a wrung out wet rag, Tilly pushed herself from the car and went inside.

Stella looked up as her daughter, with Isla trotting at her feet, entered the kitchen to the tempting aroma of baking meat. 'I didn't hear you drive in, dear.'

'I've been in the car awhile.'

Of course mothers always knew when something was amiss. Ma tilted her head and eyed Tilly wisely. 'What's wrong?' her cutting knife hovering in mid-air chopping potatoes and pumpkin to add to the roast.

After she explained, Stella gasped and set her mouth in a grim line. 'Must have been because you spoke to Sergeant John.'

Tilly grimaced. 'Actually I didn't.'

Stella scoffed. 'Matilda May Schroder! Really?'

Ma must be really angry to use her full name. 'It doesn't matter now. I think Luke did because Joe said Sergeant John paid him a visit.'

'Good for Luke. That man's grown a backbone and then some. He's a credit to Alice, rest her soul.'

Lingering in the kitchen, Tilly frowned. 'Ma, I can't deny I'm worried for us both with Joe back in town and back to his bullying tricks again. Even with Sergeant John keeping an eye out, he can't be everywhere and he's responsible for a big area.'

'He has back up from Horsham.'

'By then it might be too late. For either of us. Might not be quite so terrifying if I wasn't always facing a rifle.'

'You could carry our farm rifle in the car,' Stella suggested.

Tilly gaped. Her mother was serious! 'Ma! Leaving you defenceless?'

'Don't worry about me. I can take care of myself.'

Tilly never failed to be amazed by her mother's positive attitude. Facing life head on and getting on with the job. While Stella moved to the stove to add the vegetables to the roasting pan she had pulled from the oven, Tilly changed from her teaching clothes into jeans and a windcheater.

As they settled before the open fire waiting for dinner to cook, Isla lying at Tilly's feet, she forced herself to raise the touchy subject that had plagued her mind in recent months and weather Ma's reaction.

'Went to see Doctor Singh at the Medical Centre today.' Tilly paused to let that teaser sink in. She didn't have to wait long.

'I told you I'm fine,' Stella snapped. 'No affects from my tumble in the garden. Hardly a bruise. Just a sore backside.'

'I did mention your fall,' Tilly continued, 'then he asked if you had spoken to me about your recent appointment with him.' Naturally, Stella hadn't breathed a word so Tilly waited with interest to hear what she had to say.

'Just got the results of some tests,' she muttered. 'Told me something I already knew. I'm getting older. I need to slow down.'

'I could have told you that for free,' Tilly quipped.

She admired her mother's tireless flagging work ethic but in recent months had noticed the grimace on her tanned weathered face, the reaching out for support when she thought her daughter wasn't watching.

'You know I will always care for you.'

'But?' Stella said wryly.

'What if there comes a time when I can't and you need more.'

'Don't even mention it. I'm not ready for the Bingun Village aged care home yet and you know it.'

'Will you be honest with yourself and me if that time ever comes?' Stella didn't answer. 'Ma?' 'All right.'

For now, that grudging response would have to be enough. After dinner, although Ma protested since Tilly already had a long day teaching, another threat from Joe at gunpoint and a backlash of distress, she shrugged on her puffer coat anyway and braved the spring evening chill.

With Isla trotting at her heels, Tilly strode downhill toward the creekside fence and Luke's beckoning campfire. Best to get this challenge over with before she lost her nerve, otherwise it would bug both of them until they did.

So far, apart from her father's death two years ago, today had proved to be the most emotionally exhausting since the accident five years before. But somehow Tilly knew she wouldn't sleep properly until she dealt with this confrontation. It was clear she and Luke needed to find some kind of mutual peace and acceptance of the past since they were the only survivors of that terrifying night.

Luke obviously saw her swinging torchlight approach because he was waiting by a fence post, one booted foot pressing down a wire, a hand on the one above pulling them wider apart so she could climb through.

As she straightened up on the other side and faced him inches away, she gasped and smiled. Wow. Just, wow! His trimmed sandy hair fell in soft untidy waves and with his face no longer hidden behind its overgrown bush of long shaggy whiskers — except for an appealing shadow of stubble — Luke Hunter was a really handsome man. The boy she remembered was gone, in every way. This refreshing transformation revived the air of danger he had always possessed.

Tilly found herself staring in awe, was even drawn to feel a kick of attraction. They were the same age, after all, but she had always thought of him as being Christian's little brother.

Speechless for more than just a moment, she eventually gabbled out, 'You look amazing. What a difference.' Was there a bit too much heat in his returning gaze?

'Thanks,' he murmured, moving toward the campfire, indicating she follow.

Tilly shoved her cold hands into her coat pockets. Jolted by the power of her positive reaction to the change in Luke, she fought her thrill of amazement. 'Bet that took courage.'

He shrugged.

Isla wagged her tail and looked up at him with admiration, too.

'Hey, girl,' he said softly, bending to stroke the animal.

'I know I didn't — '

'Thanks for — '

Tilly smiled. 'You first.'

'Thanks for coming. Know it can't have been easy.'

'I've had a few light bulb moments lately. It's time.'

'Sit down.' He pointed to the log by the fire and poked at the coals, adding more wood. Sparks showered into the darkness around them. A blackened billy sang at the side of the fire. Isla yawned and stretched out at Tilly's feet.

'Can I offer you a hot drink?'

She shook her head. 'I'm fine. Just had dinner.'

Luke sat down close beside her, his hands folded between his knees, touching hers. 'I apologise for everything that happened that night. If I could change anything, I would do it like that,' he snapped his fingers.

Tilly swallowed hard. 'It wasn't your fault. You would have done the same thing for Christian if the situation was reversed. You two brothers were close. Your mother made sure of that and with good reason. Insight maybe. But that doesn't change our truth of what actually happened. Christian was driving, I was a front seat passenger and you were passed out lying on the back seat without a seat belt. The paramedics said that's probably what saved you. Being thrown clear.'

Luke groaned and shook his head. 'I shouldn't have been —'

'Don't,' she whispered, choking up. She reached out and clasped his hands in her. 'Doesn't do any good. You escaped with only slight injuries. As twisted as it sounds, be grateful for that. We all lost so much that night. People we loved, our innocence. We were all victims of a horrid tragic crash. But it was no accident,' she said fiercely, staring into the flaring flames.

She felt Luke's questioning eyes on her as he turned aside. She met his gaze. It was time he knew what she considered was closer to the truth. Confirmed, she believed, by Joe's two recent threats to her life. The cowardly old man was running scared, not game to face her without a gun. The police were breathing down his neck now so it was vital she stay alert and put some security measures in place for herself and her mother.

For tonight, it was her duty to try and break the agony it was obvious Luke unknowingly suffered.

'After the accident, I was in hospital for so long I missed Christian's funeral. But you were there.'

'We all prayed for you that day and all you lost.'

'You lost Christian too, Luke, and your mother two weeks before that.'

'I hated standing beside Joe the day of Mum's funeral,' he muttered. 'Christian was still alive then. Never hated a man so much for being a phoney weasel. Accepting all the sympathy. Pretending to be devastated by his wife's death when he treated her so mean all their married life.'

Tilly heard the anguished bitterness in Luke's voice as he spoke. Time to put forward what only she had witnessed that night. 'Luke.' She hesitated. How to phrase what she suspected? 'I have a theory. I'm not casting blame. Joe has already served time for his culpability which doesn't bring back Christian or our baby girl but I know what I saw.

'He was drunk. He rammed your car. Two lives were lost and two survived. Christian had virtually no time to react. We both saw Joe's vehicle approach from our right at the intersection but he was on a give way sign and he did slow down. For a bit. I was watching his vehicle the whole time as we drove by. What Christian didn't see, because he was focused on the road ahead and only glanced right in horror just before impact, was the look of crazy delight on Joe's face. He wasn't just mad or drunk, he was laughing.'

Luke frowned and gaped at Tilly as she spoke, shaking his head either in disbelief or disagreement.

'I clearly saw Joe through the driver side window. Looked to me like he knew exactly what he was doing because he sped up again at the last moment.'

Luke's wide eyes and scowl told her he was horrified by such a suggestion. 'Tilly that could never be proved.'

'I know. And it never will. I know he's your father but that gleam of satisfaction I saw on his face just seconds before we crashed will stay with me forever.'

'Why would Joe want to kill his own son?' Luke rasped out. 'Doesn't make sense.'

'Whether he knew it was us or not, I will always firmly believe he deliberately drove into your car.'

Luke sighed heavily, slunk forward with his elbows on his knees and pushed his hands up into his hair. 'We all know Joe. He had a temper and he used it on every member of his family. Mother more than most. But deliberately try to kill someone?'

'He's threatened me with a rifle twice this week.' It slipped out before Tilly had a chance to prepare him and check her words.

Luke whipped around to face her. 'Twice?'

She nodded. 'This afternoon on the way home from school.'

He sprang to his feet, standing astride, hands on hips, blue eyes blazing with anger. 'You okay?'

She nodded.

'What happened?'

Tilly told him, clenching her hands together to stop shaking. Repeating the ordeal only brought it all back.

Luke sat down beside her again. 'Tilly I'm so sorry. His action was unforgiveable. No consolation but at least you have it on video. You have to go to the police with it.'

'Joe said Sergeant John had already paid him a visit.'

Luke looked sheepish. 'Because of me. I called into the police station and reported the cemetery threat while I was in town this morning.'

Tilly smiled wearily. 'I thought so,' adding quickly, 'I don't mind. I should have gone in myself straight after the first time but I was so shaken. Not thinking clearly. I've been around a rifle on the farm but to have one shoved in your face. Twice,' she faltered. 'How do I protect Ma now Joe's free and loose again? Because before Dave Meyer drove up, Joe hinted I should take care of her. It was a threat.

'And you know what?' she scowled in deeper thought, 'that's what makes me suspicious about the night of the accident. For a fraction of a second through that window Joe and I saw and recognised each other. He knows I know his actions that night were deliberate. I'm a threat and he's fronted me twice to frighten me off and not say anything.'

Only when Tilly had finished talking out her thoughts did she realise Luke had gone quiet. As she blurted out her speculation, she hadn't given a thought to how he might respond. Understandable if he was feeling offended by yet another accusation against his father.

'Luke I'm just trying to make sense of it all. Trying to process that night, talk about it, analyse it and be done with it. I'm sorry to be using you as a sounding board.'

He was shaking his head. She'd gone too far! She should have kept her idea to herself. But it had helped so much just sitting here in the peaceful dark talking, trying to work it all out.

He was still silent. 'Luke? I'm sorry if — '

'No. No, it's okay.' He held up a finger as though about to point something out. After a moment, he said, 'There might be something in what you say. I'm working on a hunch, too.' He turned and looked her directly in the eye. 'I've always wondered about my mother's death. Her drowning behind the wheel of her vehicle in the dam was attributed to misadventure because no mechanical problem or other evidence was ever found as the cause to suspect otherwise. So her death was ruled as *accidental*,' he stressed with sarcasm.

'The lawyer did a good job of raising that he was drunk the night of our car crash because he'd not long lost his wife so they claimed extenuating psychological circumstances. He still

69

got a five year prison sentence for culpable driving and he deserved it because not back then and even to this day, has he ever apologised.

'I always thought the whole thing about Mum's drowning was so strange because she couldn't swim. She wouldn't have gone anywhere near the dam let alone deliberately driven into it. I know Joe was beating her up bad. Maybe it just all got to her and she decided to end it all. But Mum was made of stronger stuff. She would never go that far. Christian often told her to get out.'

'Yes, he mentioned that. I always saw Alice as a strong woman too. That's why she endured so much. She probably stayed for you boys.'

'No.' Luke was adamant. 'That's another mystery. Even before we finished school, Christian begged her to leave Joe. Told her we'd be okay. Watch out for each other.'

'And she still refused?'

'Not exactly. She said the strangest thing. *I have my reason.* I remember at the time Christian just muttered that it better be a pretty damn good one.'

'She never explained?'

He shook his head. 'Just went quiet. Looked really peaceful and accepting. Something was helping her through a tough life.'

'Her faith was strong,' Tilly suggested. 'Never missed a Sunday service. She and Ma were close but they always met in our farmhouse kitchen.' Tilly choked up and pressed a hand to her mouth at the memories, the laughter and happy times the two women enjoyed so briefly together.

'You okay?' Luke gently rubbed her back.

She nodded. 'Alice always said she was so pleased Christian and I were together. She would have been devastated to know her son and our baby were killed.'

Luke clenched his jaw. 'Joe still has so much to answer for.'

'Doesn't seem fair, huh?' Tilly grew reflective. 'I believe in karma,' she said softly.

'Let's hope it catches up with him. Even before we left school, Christian and I made a pact to stick around on the farm. Defend Mum. See how life panned out.' He paused for a frustrated sigh. 'Who knew?'

'Exactly.'

They sat in silence awhile staring into the coals, each deep in their own world of thoughts.

'By the time I was released from hospital you were already gone,' Tilly said sadly.

'Leaving — ' Luke faltered, 'Bingun was the hardest thing I ever did. My biggest regret was the day Mum died. Christian and I were working on a neighbour's farm. Joe offered us to help Dave Meyer pull down some old sheds. You always think *what if,* you know? If we'd been around.'

'Hindsight. It's a magical thing,' she said wryly, pausing. 'I've been holding onto Christian and Anna May too tight.'

It was voiced with such fragility that when Luke shuffled closer so that their bodies touched again and he spread an arm around her shoulders, words became irrelevant.

She found the realisation and confession

challenging, especially in front of Luke who she was finding alarmingly easy to talk to. In the past, she had misjudged him, building up an emotional barrier, choosing to lay at least partial blame against him for that night. But she had been wrong and knew that had been a misguided injustice.

Dryness choked her throat and tears pooled in her eyes. 'Doesn't mean I didn't love them or that I'll forget them. They're with me forever. But it has held me back from moving on.' She turned to Luke. 'You're the reason I've been prompted to face my fixed mindset. In a positive way. You were equally affected by the accident and you coming home has forced me to properly deal with that crazy happy and sad time in our past. Just seeing you and hearing your story and how we've both struggled with the hurt.'

'Pleased to hear it.'

She drowned in the depth of compassion flooding those blue eyes. 'Scary to contemplate,' she admitted with a weak smile, rubbing her hands nervously along her jeans.

'I know what you mean.'

Tilly studied him. Once, Luke had plenty of casual girlfriends but never anyone serious. Had he met a woman while he was away? 'You do?'

'Sure.'

'You've known someone special?'

'In a fashion.'

She itched to know when and where but decided not to probe. To explore it now didn't feel right. Maybe another time. 'It's like an awakening. That I should be open to a second chance even if it never comes along.' When Luke pulled that familiar and easy disarming grin, Tilly was intrigued. 'What?'

'Tilly Schroder,' he chuckled low and soft. 'You're a beautiful kind woman. That's why Christian snapped you up. You underestimate yourself.'

Tilly felt herself flush hot at his flattery and it wasn't from the campfire's radiant heat keeping them toasty warm. 'Thanks,' she murmured, confused.

She hadn't received such a humble bonding compliment in a very long time and certainly not from another man, although one or two locals had tossed out a few hints over the years which she promptly ignored. What if one of them was a missed opportunity? She tried to remember who but failed. Too late now.

Luke removed his arm and playfully nudged her shoulder. 'We can't change the past but we can do something about our future.'

'True. It's been good to talk about it. Sorry I couldn't do it sooner. I wasn't ready to remember the people we loved and lost. Now I know not to dwell on it so it affects the present. I'm finding that the hardest thing to do.' She waited a heartbeat. 'Did you ever get lonely while you were away?'

'Couldn't afford to.'

'What kept you going?'

Luke sent her an odd side glance. 'If I'm honest, remembering home.' He didn't elaborate but Tilly thought she understood. 'Looks like you're settled in Bingun too.'

She shrugged and stared up across the paddock toward the farmhouse lights. 'For now. I'm here for Ma but I want to stay. Christian and Anna May and Dad are all buried here. That's a tough link to break.'

'I'm always here for you,' he offered quietly.

'I know. I guess you don't plan on returning to the farm.'

'Hell no. Never.'

She glanced around at his humble campsite. A small overnight pitched tent and an open fire. 'You can't live here permanently.'

He shrugged easily. 'It'll do for now. Might even have a job soon, thanks to Josie.' Tilly raised her eyebrows. 'Possibly truck driving for the grain company.'

'Great. Come harvest there'll be no shortage of work and you have the experience.'

For the first time in a while during their conversation, an awkward moment slid between them. Tilly stood and looked down at him, his newly-styled golden hair shining in the firelight. Once, he was almost her brother in law. Now? She believed they had forged a new friendship and understanding with a completely different perspective and connection. As two individuals moving forward, finding their way and watching out for each other.

She sank her hands into her puffer coat pockets. 'Sorry I wasn't able to talk to you before now but after Joe today — '

'Don't need to apologise. I get you.' Luke rose and stepped closer, gently rubbing her arm.

'Facing fate makes you stop and think.' She

studied the soft expression on his face. Those blue eyes were surely powerful but also made her feel comfortable and secure. Safe. Which is why she took a pace closer, confident enough to suggest, 'Mates?'

'Sure.'

Tilly smiled and, on impulse, reached out to wrap her arms around his neck in a hug. 'Thanks for tonight,' she began to pull away.

Before Luke released her, he pressed a warm lingering kiss to her forehead. He felt muscled and strong but his tender gesture took her by surprise.

As she moved away and Isla lazily rose to trot after her, Luke followed too and said, 'I'll hold the fence for you.'

She laughed as she snapped on her torch, feeling spoilt. 'I'm a country girl, remember?'

'Noted,' he flashed a larrikin smile, 'but I aim to treat a woman right.'

Not all sons repeated the sins of their fathers, Tilly reflected with respect. Christian hadn't either. It had taken Luke a while longer but both sons had done their mistreated mother proud. Her body hummed with warmth at the knowledge. Again, she sensed that hint of something more than personal in Luke's deep voice and wondered.

After she scrambled through the fence, he grew serious. 'Take care out there.'

A warning? 'If you mean Joe, I will.' She waved, turned away and headed back to the house.

Tilly couldn't nail exactly what her intuition was telling her about Luke but his manner was beyond familiar. It was almost . . . intimate. Was he hitting on her? Attracted maybe?

And how did she feel about that?

As she strode uphill, her mind buzzed with crazy possibilities and the newness of it all. Probably just the familiarity of seeing him again, prompting old feelings and memories.

Taking her back in time. Reminding her the Schroder women needed to put some security strategies in place against the drunken old crook who was seriously disturbing their life right now.

6

Luke doused the low embers in his campfire and zipped up his tent, about all he could do to safeguard his few worldly possessions, trusting the honesty of locals and the fact that the swamp reserve was secluded.

He was not anticipating today's meeting. Had postponed it until he felt ready but after Tilly's unexpected visit last night and the revelation of Joe's second armed confrontation yesterday, it was time. The old man had forced his hand.

He shrugged on a puffer vest over his warm shirt against the still fresh spring morning, raked a hand through his short hair — still a novelty — and strode along the track to Swamp Road. From there it was a brisk hike past Schroder's place to the Hunter farm.

Even scouring the property from a distance wasn't encouraging. The front gate sagged off its hinges and he sidestepped the potholes in the dirt road. What had once been a respectably maintained façade under his mother's dedicated labours, the weatherboard house no longer bore any signs of comfort or pride. Standing back, feet astride and hands on hips, Luke stared at the derelict vision and dead garden.

Joe's ute was parked at the front steps. No dogs barked to warn of his arrival and a rifle leaned against the wall by the scratched and unpainted front door. Fair enough, no one had lived here for five years but the old place carried the neglectful scars of its alcoholic owner.

Luke took the creaky steps up to the veranda assuming Joe was possibly still sleeping off the drink. That night five years ago had taught him the value and fragility of life. Whether lost or saved. He grieved and missed the comradeship of a brother and warmth of his mother, both taken far too soon.

But equally and selfishly, every day sent a prayer of thanks for the deliverance and safety of the woman he has always adored.

He didn't bother to knock and entered, surprised to find his father sitting at the kitchen table and, from the strong aroma, drinking coffee.

The room's untidy shambles hit Luke hard. When his mother was alive it shone, everything had a place. Aromas invaded your senses even as your boots stepped onto the veranda and before you had opened the door. Into the warm heart of the home.

No more. Those days were gone.

Joe's bleary gaze rose to meet Luke's. 'This ain't your home anymore,' he growled.

'I know it.' Luke reined in his anger and disgust, shifting straight to the point of his visit. 'You keep threatening Tilly and you'll end up back in prison.'

'Only cowards obey the law,' Joe muttered. 'Someone turned me in,' he glared with venom.

'Wasn't Tilly,' Luke said quietly. 'It was me.'

'Why?' the old man snarled.

Luke almost laughed in his face. 'With good

78

reason. You held a rifle to the woman. Twice.'

'Wrong one again,' Joe mumbled, slurping up the dregs of his coffee.

Luke scowled. 'What do you mean?'

Joe's eyes narrowed and he smirked. 'Never you mind. Just git. You're not welcome here anymore.'

Luke nodded, glad to leave. 'My pleasure, but you stop harassing Tilly,' he warned. 'She's never done you wrong. She was engaged to your son and about to gift you the blessing of a grand-child.' He paused to let his words sink in. 'Leave her be. Understand?' Luke lowered his voice and stared Joe down. The old man pierced him with a challenging silence. 'You hurt or threaten her in any way again and I'll personally find you and make you pay.'

'You got no power over me, boy.' He raised his croaky voice and shouted, 'I said git. You ain't my son.'

Luke had heard all that bluster before. He wasn't hearing anything new. Yet, despite wandering alone for years, it still stung to be disowned.

He took one quick final glance around the room, equally grateful his mother wasn't around to witness her prized domain reduced to a hovel but also wishing in vain that she was still alive. He'd give anything to have her back, see her gentle smile, and never thought he'd ever stop feeling a weight of guilt for not being here when she needed him most on the day she died. An ongoing struggle in his head against it.

Luke felt no emotion as he turned and walked away, keen yet sad to leave. Unless Joe's actions demanded it, he never wanted to return.

He didn't give a damn what happened to the farm. It could rot. The place held more bad memories than good so he clung to those passable times with images of his loyal older brother and kind hearted long-suffering mother.

★　★　★

Friday. As much as she loved teaching, Tilly usually craved weekends. Being one week shy of end of term meant grading subjects and writing reports for her students. So a box on the back seat of her sporty SUV was filled with folders and potential work over the weekend.

Chloe Bennett's behaviour was still anxious but no worse. Perhaps the coming holidays would be the break she needed to help turn around her concerning anxiety. Which Tilly discovered today wasn't only for the girl herself. After class this afternoon, Chloe lingered and approached her alone once everyone else had left.

She still recalled the girl's white face and nervous manner. 'Are you okay, Miss Schroder?' she had asked in a small voice.

A puzzled Tilly didn't know where the conversation was heading or what the girl referred to so, believing she needed reassurance in some way, said warmly, 'Yes, I'm fine, Chloe. Thanks for asking. End of term's always a busy time, isn't it?

Chloe frowned. 'Oh, I didn't mean school. Mum said Mr. Hunter held you up with a rifle.'

Tilly well knew that in a small town and close community, matters didn't always stay private for long. From one person to the next, who knew someone else, word escaped and rumours spread. So she grew concerned that this news might only add to Chloe's problem. Her mother, Karen, had already mentioned Chloe's fear of Joe Hunter, understandable considering his past crimes, but Tilly desperately wished she knew why it appeared to affect the girl much more personally and deeply.

'Well, yes, he did but sadly Mr. Hunter is a troubled man who drinks. He's had a hard life and that affects him. Doesn't excuse his behaviour. As you know he's already been to prison for a reckless driving mistake.'

Chloe nervously twisted her hands together. 'But he's out of prison now and doing bad things again.'

'He's been reported,' Tilly explained carefully. 'The police know and are watching him.'

'But what if that isn't enough and he uses his rifle again?'

Tilly went cold. Chloe spoke as if she had been there and witnessed it herself. 'He won't harm you, Chloe. You're perfectly safe. Do you want me to walk with you out to the car to your mother?'

The girl nodded. Tilly moved slowly and spoke gently as they packed up her backpack and headed for the carpark pickup together.

'Okay if I have a word to your Mum?'

Chloe nodded and climbed into their four wheel drive.

'Hi Karen.' Tilly lowered her voice as they spoke near the car. 'Chloe was really upset about my recent *incident* with Joe Hunter. I've tried to reassure her. Just thought you should know.'

Karen sighed, frowning. 'Thanks, Tilly.' She glanced back toward the vehicle and a distraught daughter watching them from inside. 'She's been really edgy. It's not easing off like it usually does in previous years. Joe Hunter's actions are really making her fearful. She won't let me out of her sight. Since it's nearly the end of term and school's winding down before the holidays, I even considered keeping her home with me.'

Tilly nodded. 'Do that if you feel it will help. Has she ever said why she's so afraid of Joe?'

Karen shook her head. 'She refuses to talk about it but it's connected to about the time of Alice Hunter's death. Chloe is terrified of driving along Swamp Road now and passing the property so that's why we don't use the bus and I drive the kids to school now. Mrs. Hunter's death was horrible and tragic but it has really affected Chloe deeply yet she won't say why.'

'If I can help in any way, let me know,' Tilly offered earnestly.

'Of course. Thanks. I've suggested counselling to get to the bottom of it but she won't even agree to sessions or at least going to meet with someone. We've tried.'

'Chloe's one of my top students, Karen, so keep her home if you want. We're only doing the Aged Care home visit next week that she won't want to miss. She always looks forward to that and chatting to the residents.'

As Tilly recalled the concerning chat with Chloe and Karen Bennett driving home, she gradually eased her thoughts away from schooling to how she could put extra safety precautions in place against Joe Hunter, the cause of so much ongoing trouble and upset in the district right now. The past was still haunting so many people even in the present. Tilly wondered how on earth the upheaval would all work itself out. Please God not with any more *accidents* or lives lost.

She puzzled over what would make her feel more reassured about Stella. Older and more isolated, she would more likely succumb to physical acts of violence or threats. Was less able to defend any assault during the week while Tilly was absent and Ma alone. Like it or not, they needed to have a serious conversation on the issue.

Although Joe was dangerous and unstable, oddly, Tilly held no great fear for her own safety. The best she could come up with for now was to maybe phone their neighbours to make them aware of the situation. Luke, her fellow teachers at school and Sergeant John were already informed.

Both she and Stella already carried their mobiles on them at all times, Ma only as a result of Tilly's persistent nagging. She had called into the police station and reported Joe's latest offence which no doubt meant another official visit to the Hunter farm and involving Dave Meyer to provide a witness statement.

More worrying was always the raised risk of Joe's revenge again. A man with a wild nature and violent temper to match. A reckless character whose prison sentence Tilly considered way too lenient for his crime. And that was only the one they knew about. She would bet there were more and few locals would disagree.

As Tilly turned down Swamp Road, her thoughts were drifting toward a beer and what she had planned for dinner when her vehicle crested a rise to see a man running flat out along the roadside ahead.

Luke?

It only took a moment to see why. A thick drift of smoke and flames in the distance. At his campsite! Damn.

Tilly almost braked to a halt as she came up alongside him and, while the car slowly rolled, he grabbed the door, wrenched it open and jumped in.

'There's a bucket in the boot. I'll stop at the farm and you can drive this down to your camp first. I'll hook up the water tanker trailer to the ute and be down in five minutes.'

'My campfire was out,' Luke ground out, scowling. 'There's no wind.'

At the gate, Tilly stopped, leapt out so Luke could change places and jump behind the wheel, then ran for the open fronted machinery shed this side of the house. Isla waited as usual and raced at her side, barking.

'Isla, stay!' The dog looked bewildered but obeyed. 'Good girl.'

Tilly hooked up the water trailer, grabbed the ute keys from the sun visor and within minutes was making dust. She didn't like their chances. That fire already looked ferocious. Strange when the winter green grass would be cool and damp from the gum trees shading the swamp campsite.

84

Must have been burning awhile because if she wasn't mistaken, Tilly peered ahead, Luke's tent was well alight. Fire must have jumped the distance between the fireplace and his camp.

As she pulled up, it looked like Luke had given up on fighting the fire. He was wrapped in his big overcoat, trying to drag his belongings from the flaming tent.

Tilly shook her head and gasped as she turned on the water motor and started dragging the hose toward the fire. She knew any blaze could be unpredictable especially ahead of a wind but how the hell had the fire skipped from the pit to Luke's camp on a calm day? The grass in between wasn't burnt. It was still green. Far too early in the season for any hot days to dry out the vegetation and turn brown. A spark wouldn't spit that far if the coals were out as Luke claimed.

She trained the water on the flaring remains of the tent. Tilly didn't like the way Luke darted around the licking flames but at least he'd worn his coat for some protection and managed to save his sleeping bag and esky.

Tilly had helped fight a few grass and farm fires in her time but her throat tightened and her heart pounded erratically until the fire was out and Luke appeared safe.

'Damn,' she heard him mutter as she stopped the hose and strode closer.

'You okay?'

He nodded. 'Didn't have time to bucket water. Tent went up like paper.' He glanced around the blackened debris of his small camp and paced.

'Those coals were out when I left and this tent didn't light itself.' Suspicion rose in her mind even as Luke said with firm conviction, 'This fire was deliberately lit and, judging by the fumes from the unburnt grass, helped along by some petrol. Guess who?'

Tilly backed up and leant against the front of the ute, shaking her head. 'He's crazy.' She paused. 'You didn't rescue much.' Her gaze scanned their surroundings and she filled with a sense of helpless fury.

'Didn't have much to lose,' he said quietly. 'Thanks, mate. We tried.'

'Sorry I wasn't more help.'

'Nothing we could have done.' He lazily surveyed her slacks, smart shirt and chunky low heels from head to toe and quipped, 'You usually dress up for fighting fires?'

Tilly closed her eyes for a moment and then smiled. 'Only in emergencies.'

She used the short break in their conversation to study Luke and could only imagine what frustrations raced through his mind. Outwardly he didn't seem angry but he must be feeling beat and hopeless. Yet had somehow dredged up that larrikin humour she remembered.

'Well,' she sighed, 'unless you plan on sleeping under the stars you can't stay here.'

'Done it before,' he shrugged.

'Luke,' her gaze begged him to be practical, 'you know our spring is wind and rain. Be two months before any settled weather and summer heat.'

She had an idea but would he agree?

Travelling solo in recent years, the man might have needed to be independent in the past. But he was home now. In Bingun among friends and neighbours. Comes a time when it was okay for a body to accept a helping hand so she went for it anyway.

'Our mudbrick cottage up near the house will be dusty but it's empty,' she suggested easily without any hint of pressure in her voice. 'Happy to clean it up if it's a possibility for you.'

She waited, noting the reluctance. His hesitation either meant he was tempted or, for whatever reason, thinking how he could politely refuse.

Sneaky enough to offer an incentive, she added, 'Renovated a few years ago. Not five star digs but it's actually liveable now. Open fire, table and chairs, and a bed.'

Luke scratched his head, embarrassed. Cute. She stopped a smile and slid in, 'Don't know what your long term plans are but since you have a job you'll be here awhile. Save time looking around for something else, huh?' She shrugged and turned to leave. 'All yours if you want it.' Then deliberately changed the subject, 'I'll take the car back to the house if you wouldn't mind driving up the ute and trailer. I'll unlock the cottage and you can check it out. No strings,' she called over her shoulder with a grin.

Of course the bonus of having Luke closer to the farmhouse, Tilly realised as she drove home, even for some of the time, was that extra security she had been thinking about for herself and Ma, and another pair of eyes around the place.

In the end, Luke caved. Privately delighted,

somehow Tilly knew he would.

'To be honest,' he admitted later when they were jammed together and almost filled the compact single room in the cottage, 'be nice to have a roof and stay more than a few days or weeks in one place.'

'Apparently this was my great grandparents' first home,' Tilly glanced around with affection. 'Dad's grandparents, Albert and Emily Schroder. Water and power are connected. A workman used it for a while before Dad died,' she revealed. 'Pleasure to share it with you.' She pressed her hand against a thick wall. 'If only these could talk,' she murmured, more for something to say and fill the heavy awkwardness hovering between them as they stood close.

Feeling excited yet uncomfortable, Tilly stepped away, turning for the open door. 'I'll leave you to get settled. You know you're welcome to share our evening meal.'

Luke shook his head. 'Thanks but I prefer to be independent for now.'

She tried not to be disappointed knowing she was afraid of spending too much time around him. 'Sure. I'll scrounge some old pots for cooking. Take what you need from the wood heap. I could probably dig out an old microwave from the store shed if it helps?'

'Wood fire will be fine.'

'You can use the bathroom up at the house.'

'Thanks.'

Tilly hesitated. Should she? 'Nice to have you back, Luke,' she admitted softly. It was, and he seemed pleased to hear it.

Luke didn't know how much longer he could hold out. He desperately wanted to touch Tilly, feel her body and skin, squeeze her tight in his arms and kiss her until they were both steamed and breathless. A man could tell when a woman was interested. After a lifetime of waiting he finally had Tilly's attention, a gift too precious to misuse. He knew he had her thinking so he just needed to dig up the courage to make that first move. He didn't want to rush her. While Christian was alive she had belonged to him body and soul to the core for life. That his brother was snatched from her and she also lost their baby was too cruel.

Emotionally, it was a mountain to climb. He'd had one too but felt like he was on the downhill run now. He might just wait a while longer, see how she responded to a bit more casual physical contact. Kinda take advantage of any close natural moments that happened along.

7

Saturday mornings, Tilly usually slept in but it was barely daylight when she heard the thump of an axe. She crept from bed, drew aside the curtain and peered out.

Luke was making easy and short work of splitting the wood pile. With his sleeves rolled up he sure had some impressive muscles. The fuel box on the veranda was full again and he wheeled a barrow load down to the cottage for himself.

Bit of a treat having a man around the house. Tilly usually struggled with the axe, leaving the wood in bigger logs for the open fire, grateful for electric cooking.

She was seeing Luke in a whole new light, almost as if he was another man from only a few short years ago.

Tilly idled over breakfast with Ma then slipped on jeans and an over shirt, bundling up her long blonde hair in a pile on her head before striding across the yard to feed the chooks and hunt for eggs, Isla never far away.

Smoke lazily rose from the cottage chimney. Last night she had been curious enough to glance out across the yard to see lights glowing from its two small windows. It was comforting knowing Luke was close by from a safety viewpoint but troubling knowing he was effectively homeless, although he seemed to bear that load well enough on his broad shoulders.

Later, redirecting her focus, she stripped the bedroom linens and towels, loading the first wash and starting the weekly house clean. Later after lunch, she and Ma would make up a shopping list and enjoy a jaunt into town together to the IGA, a cuppa at Irma's cafe, maybe taking the long way home. Especially this time of year when the last of the wattle's golden glow still shone in the bush and wildflowers started appearing among the grasses. By late afternoon, small mobs of kangaroos would emerge from shelter to graze before dusk. Usually around certain stands of gum trees close to open country, scratching their rumps, heads held high and alert.

Before heading into town, Tilly helped Ma plant out the tomato seedlings then picked a basket of fresh vegetables and delivered them down to Luke, sitting outside in the sunshine on a cottage chair, his long legs stretched out, his big old hat pulled down over his eyes.

A dreamy sight. Heart-warming to see the man relaxing, making himself at home.

'My first visitor,' he murmured, his deep voice loaded with humour as he pushed the hat back up onto his head and rose to his booted feet.

'Just brought you some produce from Ma's garden. Go help yourself when you need it. Always something growing.' Why was it so hard to sound casual? She swallowed over her dry throat before adding, 'Ma and I are driving into Bingun now. Anything we can pick up for you?'

She hesitated to invite him along. Being absent all week teaching in town, weekends were usually sacredly reserved for Tilly and her mother. While they only had each other, but life was changing.

'Have everything I need right here,' he drawled, holding her gaze, hands on hips, legs astride.

Tilly set down the basket. There it was again. That flirtation and those blue eyes searching deep into hers before taking the liberty of wandering lazily all over.

She didn't mind a man's attention. Was woman enough to recognise it and had been flattered on occasion since Christian. She might have even encouraged it if she'd felt that familiar and special pull of attraction again.

Like she was discovering with Luke. Except, this time, she was slowly beginning to understand it was a whole different connection forming with him now from the man always previously in the background of her only serious love affair with his brother.

Because Christian was no longer here. That reality suddenly hit her. Despite trying lately since the anniversary of the accident and Luke's reappearance, she still felt emotionally anchored to the past yet knew she was physically free.

'We're making pizzas for tea. Join us?' she invited with cheeky warmth, pushing herself to cherish Christian and Anna May and her memories but also testing out what it felt like to be teased by playfulness and reach out again.

He nodded and didn't need to smile. His eyes sparkled with affection, his body wired but holding back.

'Any time around dark,' she waved and walked away.

Breathe, Tilly, she repeated all the way back up to the house. What was happening?

★ ★ ★

Pizza night turned out to be fun. Luke smiled that stunning smile, which charmed Stella and melted Tilly's heart, erasing at least some of her lingering reservations. For now, anyway.

With him living in the cottage closer to the farmhouse, she decided to delay putting further safety tactics in place, especially since she had failed to figure out any other steps of protection.

There really wasn't a lot else they could do. Just remain careful and vigilant. Sergeant John was a phone call away but his beat covered the whole shire so he could be anywhere in a radius of thousands of square kilometres.

In honest discussions by the open fire after dinner later, Luke pointed out that if his camp-fire destruction was an example and Joe's fault as they suspected, the old man was probably not physically targeting. Maybe just trying to frighten them and disrupt their lives in other ways.

When Stella raised the fact that Luke had no vehicle and offered the ute, Tilly knew the offer came from her mother's innate generosity but fiercely objected. 'Ma, that would leave you stranded!'

'Joe could confront us out in the garden, down the paddock, anywhere,' she waved an arm, 'and neither the ute nor a phone would be much help then, would it?' Stella pointed out.

'Luke, when do you start work?'

'Next week but don't worry about transportation. While I was in town I spoke to Nev Reed at the garage. I can use his old Monaro after he's done a bit more work on it.'

Seemed their difficulties were sorted.

★ ★ ★

By late Sunday, although Tilly buried herself in completing her school student reports for a couple of hours, she was beyond restless. Aware of Luke's every movement around the farm. Helping Stella in the garden, chopping more wood, watching her beloved Isla defect and trot down to the cottage to investigate its new resident. Lapping up the attention from a pair of big strong hands when given, Tilly noted, and stretching out her paws by her new master's big feet.

Enticed by the sudden burst of late September sun and bugged by cowardly thoughts of escape, Tilly donned her leggings and sneakers, firmly clamped on her straw hat and headed down the farm track to Swamp Road. A decent run always cleared her head. Being an only child she had always been content in her own company, yet with Luke she fought her enjoyment around him.

In time, after an hour, the exercise wore her out but didn't really help. Her thoughts kept drifting in one direction. The subtle lift of his eyebrows in amusement. The way she caught him glance sideways at her for long intense moments. His sheer physical strength and disturbing presence. Her own private dilemma as to why she felt so bothered by his interest. Wanting to openly respond but afraid.

With a different man and in different circumstances, she might feel merely flattered by his attention. Difficult to admit but, fact was, the appreciation was mutual. When they looked at each other, it triggered a flare of curiosity and heat in her.

Roll on tomorrow and another school week. The last before spring holidays. Heavens. Her mind buzzed. She would be home and around the farm full time for two weeks. Tilly didn't know if her greatest emotion was a kick of excitement at the possible adventure life promised to be if she let her feelings grow for Luke, or butterflies of dread that she had the liberty of taking that first serious leap since Christian and could free fall without a net.

She well knew from her previous passionate love how easy that first step could be if you just took it and went with your heart.

Could she do it again?

Once, it had been so simple. Now, Tilly felt as though she hadn't earned the right after years of survivor guilt cramming her mind and stopping her from trying again. Believing she didn't deserve another shot at happiness.

As the sun lowered toward the horizon and dusk settled like a calming haze over the countryside, the early evening chill caressing her bare arms and legs, Tilly jogged in through the farm gate, grateful Luke was nowhere in sight and no lights yet shone from the cottage windows. Feeling like a coward, she snuck inside.

After a hot shower and change into comfy clothes, Tilly went to find and feed Isla, not usually missing at this time of day. Surely her darling dog wouldn't be off somewhere with Luke? The ultimate embarrassment when she had hoped to avoid him.

'You seen Isla, Ma?' Tilly called out to her in the kitchen from where she filled the feed bowls in the utility room.

'No dear. She's been out awhile now. Might have sniffed out a rabbit. You know how excited she gets.'

'Sure.'

So Tilly went outdoors again and resigned herself to whistling and calling for Isla. The dog rarely went missing but this time she just knew if the Sheltie had followed Luke it would mean facing him again when she was so reluctant. Yet could imagine what it might feel like to be held and thoroughly kissed again by any man but Luke Hunter in particular.

She retraced her footsteps along the property driveway out to Swamp Road. Isla was unlikely to have strayed off the farm and certainly not far from it. Husky voiced from calling out, Tilly was jogging back toward the farmhouse when, off to her right, she noticed Luke striding toward her out from the deepening shadows of gum trees down by the swamp, swinging a fishing rod and tackle box. He had obviously raided the store shed. No one had used the gear since her father died.

Her heart skipped a beat at the sight of him when he smiled.

Perhaps because she didn't return it, he asked, 'Anything wrong?'

'Probably not — Isla's missing.' Frowning, she looked off into the distance. 'Unlike her to go out fossicking and disappear even when she's off the lead. I've trained her to stay close. Hasn't had her usual appetite lately but its dinner time so she should be back.'

Stella emerged onto the veranda as Tilly and Luke walked toward the house. 'Evening Lucas.'

'Stella.'

'No luck yet, dear?' she asked her daughter.

Tilly shook her head. 'Might keep looking until dark. I haven't scouted this home paddock down to the creek yet.'

'I'm on it,' Luke offered.

'I'll head over to the crop paddock. If we don't find her soon, I'll try further afield in the ute.'

Luke nodded to the mobile phone in Tilly's hand. 'Want to AirDrop your number in case we find anything?'

Tilly was jolted by the request. His suggestion meant something may have happened to Isla which her mind refused to consider. She pulled a shaky smile. 'Of course.'

Stella handed them each a powerful flashlight and they set off in opposite directions.

Tilly walked aimlessly until her legs hurt striding over crop rows, her throat went dry from yelling and her arm ached from scanning around with the heavy light. With her fear growing and darkness already fallen, Tilly knew they could have missed Isla anywhere already if she was lying injured, or worse.

To cover more ground, they would need the ute. She had just turned to head homeward, using the distant farmhouse lights as a compass, when her mobile rang.

She checked it. Luke. 'Have you found her?'

The pause before he answered told her heaps. 'Yes but she's weak. I'll bring her back.'

Tilly ran and stumbled and almost fell on the uneven ground. In Luke's flashlight off to her left as he strode purposefully back to the house, she noted an unmoving Isla in his arms. She felt stifled. Isla was her child. Her baby. 'She's not-?'

Luke shook his head but even in the semi darkness she could see his expression was bleak.

Ma, bless her, had driven the ute up to the house. Tilly punched in the vet's number in Horsham and paled at the sight of her unresponsive pet. After a terse call she hung up and slid in behind the wheel, Luke nursing Isla alongside.

'Is she hurt? Injured? What's wrong?'

'Not looking good,' Luke murmured in warning as they began the twenty minute drive.

Tilly grew terrified they wouldn't make it in time.

'She was vomiting and staggering when I found her.'

Tilly moaned.

'Do you keep pest control poison or antifreeze anywhere she could get at it?'

A distraught Tilly frantically shook her head. 'No. Keep them locked up in the shed.'

She kept her focus on the night driving and dared not glance at Isla, clearly seriously ill.

Halfway there, Tilly speeding on the sealed country road, she whispered, 'Is she still breathing?'

Luke nodded.

At the vet surgery in Horsham, she parked in a rush and leapt out to race around and open the passenger door for Luke. Vet Tom was waiting but Tilly was barely able to greet him, choked up with emotion, fearing the worst, her mind blurred with panic.

Everything happened with professional efficiency. Tom took control, his calm voice asking questions, talking them through proceedings. But Tilly could clearly see it was hopeless right from the start. Isla was bleeding, losing control of her body. With her organs shutting down, Tom gently suggested euthanasia as the only humane measure to ease her suffering.

Tilly wept as Isla died, Luke's strong arms holding her tight. For quite some time she was inconsolable. Her beautiful friend and Christian's gift, gone.

She quietly sobbed all the way home, Isla wrapped in her arms, Luke driving.

'Tom said it was definitely poison,' he murmured as they finally drove through Bingun and reached the farm.

Numb, Tilly couldn't get her head around that and didn't reply. Suspicion lay unspoken between them. Stella guessed the moment her daughter stepped from the ute carrying a lifeless Isla. Luke gently took the animal so Tilly and her Ma could hug.

On the way home, he had offered to bury the

Sheltie. Now, assuming the burden, he lumbered away under the animal's weight toward the stand of gum trees where Tilly had asked that her dog be buried. Christian had proposed and gifted Isla to Tilly as a puppy there five years ago. Their special place. Tilly released a shaky sigh. She felt a mess, guessed she looked it and didn't care.

When Luke had buried Isla, he walked back up to the house. Operating on remote and with no thought being attached to any of her actions right now, Tilly moved straight for him when he returned. She had been waiting and, as his boots topped the last step, rose from the cane veranda chair to slide her arms around his waist.

'Thank you for everything,' she snuffled against him, starting to weep again.

'I'm so sorry,' he whispered, his voice rumbling against her ear as she clung to him, her head resting just below his chin, his big workman's hands caressing her back in a circle.

Mesmerised, she almost purred, their embrace and his comfort feeling like the most natural thing in the world. 'I can't go down and say goodbye to Isla tonight,' she sobbed.

'Tomorrow. Feel like food?'

'No.'

'A drink in toast to a beautiful companion?'

She nodded and pulled away to wipe her wet cheeks.

Later, knowing she was miserable company and feeling wretched over Isla's loss, Tilly excused herself and slid into bed. Burying herself beneath the covers, doubting she would sleep. Devastated with grief, already aching with longing for her beautiful Sheltie.

In the middle of the night, she woke with a start from a nightmare, sat up in bed in the dark and cursed the man responsible for her precious dog's untimely death.

8

Monday, Tilly drove on autopilot into Bingun and school. Soon after sunrise she had gathered her courage and strolled down to the trees to say a private goodbye to Isla. As she passed on her return, smoke lazily rose from the cottage chimney and she thought she saw Luke moving about inside through one of the tiny windows but he tactfully didn't appear, considerately allowing her time and space to heal. Just as well. She was a weepy mess.

School was a loud busy distraction. The morning passed with the monthly entertaining diversion of a class visit to the Bingun Village aged care home, fondly known as The Village, down the same end of town.

The children walked from the school ground, chattering about the various amusements they had organised. Reading to those with vision problems, helping residents move out to sunny spots in the gardens to play board games or simply sit and talk. Gradually also each of the willing elderly were being interviewed about their lives for a proposed school history book project.

Most children had already established a friendship with someone but Chloe Bennett always drifted, smiling, to her maternal grand-mother Helen. It warmed Tilly's heart to see the child happy and content. At least for a while, able to separate her thoughts from unpleasant brooding of late.

In a brief quiet moment of reflection, Tilly considered these caring pleasant surroundings and knew government funding was always stretched so she determined to become more involved in local fundraising efforts for The Village in future.

As Ma aged, her resistance to making the transition to such a home was concerning. Even worse if The Village was fully occupied, Stella might be faced with the very real possibility of moving to another home in another district town. Where, knowing less people, she may feel far less settled and comfortable. Many of the district elderly had lived a lifetime in the same country town, so it was often a strain and dislocation for the person and their family if they were forced to move away.

For now, Tilly couldn't even bear to consider that time. If necessary, she would stop teaching and care for Ma on the farm.

After the Village excursion, believing all the children had their usual fun time that often pro-voked interesting classroom discussions afterwards, Tilly instantly knew something was wrong for Chloe. The students had barely set foot in the school grounds again when the girl approached her in a breathless panic, hands clenched info fists.

'What's wrong, Chloe?'

'Grandma started talking today about when Mrs. Hunter died.'

Tilly privately groaned. How ironic, just when the girl had a chance to escape her personal issue, it was innocently raised again.

'And that has upset you?' Chloe nodded furiously. 'For any particular reason?' The girl nodded again, close to tears. Tilly softened her voice even further. 'How about I take you into the First Aid room and we call your Mum to come get you?'

She ushered Chloe indoors where the Principal was informed and Karen Bennett arrived from their farm fifteen minutes later.

Huddled in the room with the door firmly shut for privacy, Tilly remained at Chloe's request. *In case that man hurts you again,* the girl had said. Although she was reassured otherwise. Scary that Chloe assumed, without mentioning a name, Tilly understood who she meant.

Judging by the girl's recent troubled behaviour and present terror, whatever Grandma Helen had said may finally well be the catalyst for some kind of confession. Tilly only hoped whatever followed allowed Chloe to face the trauma so deeply affecting her life and gradually overcome her fears. Clearly connected to Alice Hunter's death.

When Chloe grew settled enough to talk, Karen gently prompted her daughter. 'So what did Grandma say that bothered you, honey?'

'That Mrs. Hunter's death wasn't an accident.'

'The verdict of the inquest and coroner's report said it was,' Karen pointed out carefully.

'Grandma said Mr. Hunter was a horrible man to Mrs. Hunter and her dying looked suspicious but no one could prove it.'

'Oh, honey,' Karen placed an arm around Chloe's shoulder, hugging her close as Tilly looked on in silent compassion, 'there's always gossip but we have to trust in the law and their investigations and decisions.'

Chloe's young eyes grew wide and she stared in fear. 'But what if somebody *did* see something?'

Karen glanced across at Tilly, their interest alerted. 'Do you know someone who did?' her mother asked. Chloe nodded. 'Was it you?'

Her daughter nodded madly again, growing more nervous and agitated as the conversation progressed in this new direction. 'Yes.' She hesitated, on the edge of disclosure, but then shook her head and began trembling. 'I saw something horrible,' she whispered and after another long pause, struggled to say, 'but Mr. Hunter said he'll come after me with his dog and his rifle and I wasn't to say anything.' She spoke so softly, Tilly barely heard. 'I'm really scared.' Chloe dissolved into sobs.

Tilly's heart privately ached for her distress. Innocent children kept secrets out of fear, believed and trusted what adults told them. Whatever Chloe saw she had been withholding in dread every single day for five long years.

'Yes you can, honey,' Karen said firmly. 'I'm your mother. I love you. You can trust me. You will not be in trouble or harmed in any way from anyone for anything you tell me now.'

Chloe sent a pleading glance to her mother. 'Promise?'

'Absolutely, honey.'

Tilly almost broke down watching the strong bonding exchange between mother and daughter with a single trusting gaze.

The conversation had turned so low and secretive as though Chloe feared being overheard. Tilly grew cold at the prospect of the possible chilling information to come. Were they about to learn some vital and previously unknown evidence about Alice Hunter's drowning death? That everyone believed to be an accident but some people suspected otherwise?

By a child. After all this time.

And then it all came tumbling out. Like a breached dam wall flooding a valley, torrents of words gushed from Chloe's mouth.

On that crucial morning five years before, six year old Chloe Bennett had been driven by her mother to the bus shelter on the road at the end of their long driveway out of the property. Karen kissed her daughter then drove off leaving an excited Chloe waiting to have a rare ride because she didn't regularly take the school bus.

Karen then drove off with her baby son, Callum, and three year old, Oliver, in their four wheel drive in the opposite direction to help in her mother Helen's medical emergency.

But the family had not known that after little Chloe waved her mother goodbye, she was already too late for the bus. Seeing no children in the bus shelter at the Bennett's gate, the new bus driver had not waited. An action for which later, deeply humbled, he would apologise and be severely reprimanded.

So Chloe had waited and waited until she knew that the bus wasn't coming today. How to get to school? With her father already gone early and her mother not at home, Chloe ran along to the next door farm to Mrs. Hunter. Even though Mr. Hunter was well known in the district for not being a very nice man, Chloe knew and trusted his wife. Puffed from running and with her backpack bouncing as she ran, Chloe turned in at the Hunter's gate and ran for the house.

'Because they lived closest on the next farm, I went to see if she could take me to school.'

As Karen pressed a shaking hand to her mouth both she and Tilly instantly knew and understood the importance of that tragic day in her daughter's life now. The fate of a resourceful country child making a decision that would change her life.

'And you didn't find her?'

Chloe looked miserable and slowly shook her head.

'What happened, honey?'

'I took the steps up onto the veranda and banged on the back kitchen door but it was quiet and Mrs. Hunter didn't answer. I peered in through a window and there were chairs turned over and it was messy, not like she usually keeps it, but there was no one inside. I was going to walk around the house to find her when I noticed Mr. Hunter down by the dam.

'He had his back turned and he was holding a rifle pointing it as though he was about to shoot. He wasn't doing anything, just standing there watching something in the water. It was Mrs. Hunter's blue car that she always drove and it was sinking and you could only see the top of it above the water. Bubbles were coming up.'

At this point, Karen and Tilly exchanged horrified glances. Tilly's suspicions and instincts had been right. It all made sense now. She raised a hand to her throat. Dear God, this child witnessed a murder and in terror kept the knowledge secret! She had seen a crime that Joe Hunter no doubt planned and did nothing to prevent. The cold blooded intent of it!

Joe Hunter would be returning to prison. For life.

After a moment, Karen prompted Chloe to continue. 'So is that when you ran back to the road and Mrs. Peterson came along in her car?'

'No. Mr. Hunter's dog saw me on the veranda and barked and ran over to the house and he snarled at me and I thought he was going to bite into me. I screamed and then Mr. Hunter must have heard because he turned around and came toward the house with his rifle aimed at me. I thought he would shoot me but he just said *What do you want, kid?*

'I told him I missed the bus and could Mrs. Hunter please drive me to school and he said she couldn't. The dog kept growling and he grabbed its collar and said I was trespassing and was to Git or he would let the dog loose on me and he didn't like visitors and I wasn't to tell anyone I'd been there.'

'So you walked back to the road, honey?'

'I ran really fast. And when I got to the road I kept running until Mrs. Peterson came along and stopped and when she got out of the car I burst out crying and just told her I missed the bus. And she said it was okay and put me in the back seat next to Tara and did up my seat belt and put my backpack in the car boot and drove me to school.'

Karen hugged Chloe tight and Tilly could see the poor mother was having trouble holding herself together, too, both women feeling distressed and angry at Chloe's ordeal and suffering ever since.

'I felt dreadful about that day,' Karen admitted, 'for rushing off in the car at the farm as soon as I dropped you off at the bus shelter. I should have waited but you were so happy to be going on the bus like a big school girl. I thought the bus would be along soon and you would be fine but my mind was distracted and so full of worry for Grandma Helen. Dad had just phoned to say Mum had an attack of some kind, the ambulance was on its way and Pete had already gone early to a property machinery sale two hours away. I was breastfeeding Callum and Oliver was still a toddler in nappies. I felt overwhelmed that morning.'

'It's okay, Mum,' Chloe said quietly to an upset teary Karen, 'you didn't know. I wanted to tell you but I knew I shouldn't and you were busy with Grandma Helen and Callum so I didn't bother. But soon everyone knew that Mrs. Hunter died by being drowned and I felt sinful because I saw what happened but Mr. Hunter told me not to say anything or he would come after me.'

Of course when confronted now he would deny it until his last breath so Tilly prayed when investigations reopened, as they surely would, the truth of Chloe's firsthand evidence with this fresh information from a key witness would be vital to the case and enough evidence to prove its truth in any new hearing. The whole situation bringing major upheaval into this quiet living country farming family and the town.

A fresh burst of hatred for Joe Hunter gripped Tilly's stomach.

What a dreadful burden this child had carried all this time. The family would need support and counselling into the future as they slowly processed and came to grips with this crisis in their lives that would affect them for a long time to come.

Not to mention what Luke would have confirmed about his own suspicions.

Karen said nothing but gathered her daughter into her arms and just held her while she sobbed her small heart out, starting to release just a small part of the load she had borne for years. The unfairness of it. Tilly pressed her lips together hard. The calculated evil of the man who would have become her father in law and the grandfather of her unborn child. If he hadn't recklessly killed his own son and future granddaughter.

Tilly reached over to grasp and squeeze Karen's hand. 'Would you like to stay here awhile with Chloe?'

She nodded. 'If you don't mind.'

Tilly held her gaze. 'I know you might not feel like eating but you've both missed lunch. How about a cuppa and a sandwich from the canteen?'

'Sure. Thanks.' Karen managed with a heavy

sigh of emotional exhaustion.

Seeing her strain, Tilly thought someone should be with them at all times, at the very least for comfort, then forced herself to pose the next logical question. 'Would you like myself or the Principal to make the phone call to Sergeant John?'

Karen reluctantly nodded her agreement but seemed relieved for Tilly to take charge. 'If you could give us some time alone together. I need to explain to Chloe the importance of all this and what happens next and phone Pete to come into town.'

'Will Dad be mad?' Chloe asked.

'No, darling,' Karen smiled weakly. 'You have no idea how proud he will be, like me, that you showed such courage to do this. What you've told us this morning is so important and everyone will be so grateful you were finally able to share what's been bothering you for so long. Mr. Hunter will go back to prison and never be released.'

'Really?' Chloe whispered, wide-eyed in surprise.

Her mother nodded. 'Where he belongs and you have played a very important part in making that justice happen.'

Karen and Chloe remained safely in the privacy of the school First Aid room awaiting the arrival of Sergeant John. In the aftermath of the girl's declaration, Tilly asked the Principal for the afternoon off and walked from the building in a daze.

In the coming days, Chloe Bennett's shocking revelation would spread like a summer wildfire through the community but Tilly wouldn't be happy until Joe Hunter was back in custody. Hopefully today after questioning. So many lives were about to be changed once the police became involved.

The past few days of a burnt out campsite deliberately destroying virtually everything a man owned in the world, and Isla's poisoning and painful end might be unproven but there was no doubt in Tilly's mind it was all the work of a demented maniac who was about to be nailed.

Grasping that rewarding knowledge, she managed to raise a satisfied smile as she drove home.

Yet her more concerned thoughts flew to Luke. How he would take this news and how his life would be affected. He might be tainted by family association. He might leave town. At that possibility, Tilly's heart skipped a beat and her spirits crumbled. Surely not? He had only just returned and she was rather liking having him around. Growing more than fond, if she was honest.

At the farm, she parked her car and marched directly for the cottage. Ma might wonder what was going on but Luke needed to be warned first and prepared for the coming situation that was about to explode. She pounded on his door and called out but dammit he wasn't there.

'Tilly?'

She spun around in the direction of the voice behind her to see him striding up from the machinery shed across the yard, wiping his hands on a rag. When he grinned, her chest

112

tightened at what she must tell him.

'Just doing some work on the Holden Monaro Nev lent me.'

A distracted Tilly, trying to be interested, glanced back over toward the sheds and noticed the familiar classic vehicle Nev kept garaged and always covered.

'Wow. Nev let you borrow his pride and joy. You'll be recognised all over the district.'

'I promised to take good care of it and help him finish the restoration.'

'Good trade,' she murmured absently, desperate to talk to him.

He paused and his grin faded as Tilly grappled with how to begin. 'What's the problem?' he scowled.

He was right. She wouldn't have returned from school this early if there wasn't one. 'Inside?'

She didn't want Ma seeing or overhearing this conversation. She would learn the awful truth about her dearest friend soon enough. Stella Schroder was a tenacious country woman but this horrific news would break her down.

Looking Luke straight in those beautiful blue eyes, as tactfully and briefly as possible, Tilly explained the gist of what Chloe Bennett had just revealed at school.

Staring at her, he swallowed hard and his tanned face paled. 'This for real?'

'Swear it.'

He blew out a deep rush of breath and bent double, planting his hands on his knees.

Close to tears, Tilly whispered, 'Luke?'

He straightened, his expression fierce. 'Why?'

Helplessly, she shrugged. They all needed the answer to that one. God she longed to reach out and hold him, offer some comfort, but now wasn't right. Maybe later if he sought it.

'Gotta be a reason,' he growled.

She nodded. There was nothing to say.

'I'm going over there to find out before the cops.' He combed his big hand roughly through his thick hair.

'Luke, don't — '

'I won't lay a hand on him. I want him to rot in gaol. Just wanna know why. Unless the man's pure evil, he doesn't do something that mean without some twisted reason in his mind.' He turned back at the door and said quietly, 'Thanks for letting me know.'

She nodded, feeling lower than bleak. Already lost and exhausted, and she hadn't even gone up to the farmhouse yet to inform her mother.

Telling Ma was worse because by then Luke had roared out of the machinery shed in Nev's classic loaner and Tilly's mind buzzed with what might be happening over at Joe's place. She hoped the confrontation didn't turn nasty and Luke got an answer. Chances were low.

Stella was rarely raised to anger but after hearing what Tilly had to say, her infuriated trembling mouth pulled into a thin line, she clenched her hands into fists and for a while didn't speak. Just sat rigid and still in her favourite chair, staring into the fire.

'Want a brandy?'

'Please.'

Tilly poured one and Ma sipped. Maybe it helped because slowly and quietly the older woman voiced her thoughts.

'This whole mess kicked into play five years ago. Alice's death and your road accident. We now know poor Alice was murdered. Joe went on a drunken spree afterwards but that was no worse than usual. Everyone around here knows that intersection is notorious. Bad enough in daytime so you take double care at night. Yet he ploughed straight into Luke's car. He must have seen the headlights coming.' She frowned, then scoffed. 'Culpable driving and prison for five years doesn't cut it with me. I lost a future son in law and granddaughter. You lost more than a fiancé and your child.'

The women shared an understanding gaze. Tilly let her mother ramble, processing her thoughts aloud.

Stella took another sip of brandy and set down her glass. 'Joe's out of prison but trouble is still going on.' She started counting on her fingers. 'Luke's camp. Isla's death. You bailed up twice at gunpoint. Whatever's gnawing at that man hasn't stopped. Joe murdered Alice and two weeks later he's responsible for the road accident. Happening so close together, you have to wonder if they're connected.'

Tilly sighed. 'Ma, we've been over all this before.'

'Not since knowing the truth behind Alice drowning.' Stella slowly shook her head. 'I can't get my thoughts around it. Why do that to an innocent woman? You know what?' It was as if she suddenly stumbled onto something and suddenly rose to face her daughter. 'I'm going to give Joe Hunter a piece of my mind.'

Tilly grew alarmed and rose beside her. 'Ma, don't even think about it. That's the brandy talking. Anyway, what's the point? He'll probably laugh in your face or curse you off the property.'

'Because Alice Hunter was my lifelong friend.' She placed a hand over her heart. 'I knew what she suffered,' her mother paused, her gaze narrowing before she finally growled, 'until her life was cut short. And now we know who was responsible.'

'I can't let you go.'

'You can't stop me, dear.'

'I'll come with you.'

'No you won't. I'll be fine. If I'm not back in thirty minutes, you can come looking for me. What I have to say to that no good, drunken, murdering son of the devil won't take long.'

'Ma, no! He's too dangerous.'

Stella held up a hand. 'I need to have my say before he's arrested. For Alice.'

'You can't. He's a murderer.'

'Joe Hunter doesn't frighten me. I've had enough.'

'Luke's already over there.'

'Then I'll stand in line and wait my turn. I'll tell you now,' Stella muttered as she left the room, 'praying for a thunderstorm and having that bastard struck by lightning and fried would be too good for him.'

Tilly didn't think anything of it when Ma seemed to take a while before she took off from the garage in the ute. She wondered if her mother was having second thoughts but as she watched her drive away, she was overcome with a bad feeling. They should all just let the police handle this. Having one last crack at a murderer was a crazy move.

Even as the ute dust faded down the gum tree drive to the road, Tilly paced and had already started worrying and watching the kitchen clock. Damn sure she wouldn't be waiting thirty minutes to follow. Her mother's life was too precious to risk.

9

As Luke rumbled in Nev's precious old wheels along Swamp Road the short distance to his father's property, he practised pulling in the explosive anger crushing his chest. His brain had pounded with disbelief after Tilly's crippling disclosure. His heart shattered for his mother to have died in such an horrific way, and for the innocence of Chloe Bennett being so cruelly stolen.

In order to try and repair the imbalance and trap Joe, he needed a clear head and calm attitude. Unlikely the law would doubt the girl's declaration but he had learned the hard way backup never hurt.

In order to carry out his game plan, he hoped Sergeant John hadn't beaten him to it. With new evidence and a firsthand witness to murder coming forward, he would probably call in city reinforcements so Luke figured he had the luxury of at least a few hours before Joe was arrested.

Laying dust, he peeled off the main road toward the sorry excuse for a farm where he used to live. It was never a home with Joe in it. His mother had been its only saving grace, each day a struggle for her to make it halfway decent, her welfare the only reason her sons stuck around. Tragically, he and Chris had failed in that goal.

Joe's ute was parked out front of the neglected

house. No sign yet of Sergeant John. Luke pulled up across the front of the vehicle in case Joe had any ideas about leaving before Luke had his answers.

Being raised in this household and the school of life had taught him to be wary. Always a time when your survival depended on it. Today was no exception. So as he left Nev's vehicle and strolled toward the house, Luke opened the voice memo app on his phone and pressed the red button, making sure to keep it in his hand near Joe so it picked up every possible word. He didn't expect the old man to confess to a damn thing but he lived in hope.

The screen door whined as it shut behind him. His booted feet echoed down the hall to the kitchen. He sent a seated Joe a silent glare, casually slid his phone onto the table beside him and sat opposite, pushing greasy plates aside to fold his hands.

Luke never expected to return here since the old man had yelled him off the place and he had been glad to leave. Joe was a wily drunk so had probably guessed any return visit had a purpose. Up front, Luke needed him to know the game was up.

'I've heard a witness has come forward claiming to have seen something the morning Mum drowned.' Joe's bleary eyes widened in shock and he squirmed in his seat, looking sick. Luke glared him down and demanded, 'What *really* happened?'

Caught off guard, the weasel turned aside to light a cigarette, stalling, but his hands shook. 'I didn't see no kid. They make up stories all the time. Fool girl's lying.'

Trapped! And he had it on tape.

Luke froze at his damning words and a lifetime of hatred and disrespect for this poor excuse of a human being rose to the fore. 'I didn't say it was a child,' he said quietly, 'or a girl.'

Chloe's story was true. She had been here on that deadly morning. And despite a brain clouded by alcohol, Joe clearly remembered, too. Which meant he was looking at his mother's murderer.

Realising his blunder, Joe yelled, spitting from the mouth with anger, 'Just because a man's been in prison now I'm gonna be accused of every little thing in the district. You got no right to cast blame. You're no son of mine. I hate the sight of you. Now git.'

'Well, I guess we'll find out what the child says soon enough. She'll be making a statement and the police will be involved,' Luke said evenly, a factor Joe would already suspect.

His beady eyes grew wide and cold and stared. Luke half turned. He reached out a hand toward his phone to turn off the recording but something made him hesitate. His old man started trembling, not from fear, Luke noticed, as his father's face grew red with rage. Bitterly, he blurted out, 'You're a bastard. Child of my fornicating wife. You're not my son.'

From his neck to his boots, Luke's whole body stiffened with shock. He watched his father lose control. Nothing new. The man had a temper anyway. But what Luke had always brushed off as Joe's usual crazy bouts of ranting anger, he now realised could possibly be the truth. All these years the old guy had been spouting accusations and everyone thought it was just the grog talking.

Joe wasn't his father?

Luke rolled the fantastic possibility around in his head. If it was true, it placed his mother in a poor light for being unfaithful. Knowing her to be a good Christian, there must be another explanation.

Before he had a chance to follow up and ask questions, Joe bellowed in agony, 'I killed the wrong one.' He bashed the table with his fist so hard cutlery rattled on the dirty plates, and the frantic man staggered to stand. He paced and muttered, pulling at his hair in distress. Suddenly, he whirled around throwing his arms in the air. 'I hate the sight of you. Git, I said. You're the spawn of the devil.'

Horrified at the depth of this man's evil, Luke urged, 'Who did you kill by mistake?'

Joe's eyes glazed over as if he was in a mental fog of his own.

Luke hardly dared voice it. 'Mum?'

The old man snapped out of his hazy stare. 'Hell no. She deserved it.'

Luke suffered an emotional punch in his gut to hear the words confirming that Joe killed his wife. Stiff with disgust, he curbed his anger and clenched his hands into balled fists to stop from lunging at this man. He silently howled like a wild animal, itching to wrap his hands around that scrawny neck and squeeze. Failing that, punch him senseless on behalf of Chris and his mother to feel better and work off his festering fury.

Luke's mind flashed back in memory. On that critical morning, Joe had claimed Alice was going into town shopping. Christian and he were already over at Dave Meyer's place helping him pull down an old stable.

Knowing what he knew now, Luke suddenly grasped the sordid truth. Nice and handy that both boys were absent while Joe planned to drown their mother. Deliberately arranged for them to be off the property that day so there were no witnesses to the crime.

But his treachery failed. A child unexpectedly appeared but, even after five years, it wasn't too late to learn the truth. Luke sent up a silent prayer that, at the time, Chloe Bennett had not been physically harmed.

However, Luke knew this wasn't the end of the afternoon's explosive revelations. There was Joe's inflammatory claim that he also killed someone else, which he said had been a mistake.

He kept his phone recording anything else Joe said to follow up his earlier admission and was about to challenge him on it but the old man's face crumpled and his watery eyes glistened.

'You should have been driving that night,' he spluttered, spittle dribbling down his chin as he spat out the words. 'I was aiming for you! You should have been driving but I killed my son instead.'

Joe killed Christian by mistake?

His brother's death was in vain?

Luke had been the target?

This despicable old creep killed two innocent human beings out of revenge? So, what, he rid himself of the woman who wronged him and then bungled getting rid of the son Alice bore?

The double blow hit Luke like a bomb. This whole situation was scarcely imaginable. His head pounding with all the lies now exposed. His mother unfaithful. The man he always knew as his father a murderer. Twice over.

Wily Joe saw Luke churning over the wild family truths. He sneered. 'Whadya think of your mother now, laying with another man behind my back while I was away shearing? Musta beat her too hard because she told me a few weeks before she died that you weren't my son.' He sniggered. 'But she didn't git the better of me. No one gets the better of Joe Hunter. I made sure she paid for what she did. A body will do anything at the point of a gun.'

A speechless seething Luke imagined how that might have progressed. His mother with a rifle aimed in her direction forced into the car and told to drive into the dam. When they all knew Alice couldn't swim.

The two men glared daggers at each other. Luke's only consolation in all this shock and upheaval was knowing Joe's entire admission had been recorded. His gut boiled with a deep dose of revulsion for a man he'd had to endure in his life who wasn't his father. If Joe wasn't, who was? Still rocked with confusion, he wasn't about to humiliate himself by asking and was amazed Joe hadn't already gloated. To make Luke suffer?

Luke's brain kicked into overdrive and his

memories of five years ago came rushing to the fore. Why his humble long suffering mother Alice had really died. Two weeks later, Joe's retribution and Christian's unintentional futile death.

Joe had always claimed that ramming Luke's car with Christian driving and a pregnant Tilly in the front passenger seat beside him was really just his drunken state and caused by grief over the death of his wife. Which it was now revealed Joe had contrived himself!

At the time, Joe had been given the benefit of the doubt. Luke remembered those words *extenuating circumstances*. With no evidence to convict him, district folk and the law attributed two tragic road deaths as accidental, caused by Joe Hunter's mental breakdown over his wife's death.

What a bullshit joke! Luke burned with a rage he had trouble reining in. Up to this day in his life, it was the hardest thing he had to do, but Luke ground his jaw and retrieved his still-recording phone.

As Luke picked it up, Joe snapped, 'Who you calling?'

'No one,' he growled low and threatening. 'No need. You'll be in handcuffs soon enough. Meantime, squirm you bastard. You're freedom's over. You're heading straight back to prison and never getting out.'

Sitting in Nev's Monaro, his hands loosely hanging over the top of the steering wheel, Luke took a second to clear his head, enough to drive.

Back out on the road, he gunned the engine which responded like a dream but he had no idea where he was heading and didn't care.

Tilly grew more anxious with every single one of the thirty-five long minutes her mother was away. Just knowing the fragile woman so dear to her heart was in the presence of that evil neighbour was enough to give a person palpitations. So when she heard the throaty note of Nev's Monaro rumble along the driveway and pull up outside the cottage, she raced across the yard to meet Luke.

'Did you see Ma?'

In her fear for Stella, she didn't immediately register his hunched shoulders and lined brow of exhaustion.

'No. I was only with Joe for fifteen minutes, then I've been . . . driving.'

'Oh.'

Tilly finally noticed Luke's mood. Usually smiling and upbeat no matter what, he slumped against the sporty vehicle and stared off into the distance. She longed to reach out and brush back some of that thick sandy hair off his forehead. The conversation with Joe for such an appalling purpose was never destined to go well.

'You missed Ma, then. I was hoping — '

'What?' Luke became alert again and paid attention.

'Ma went to see Joe. I thought you might have seen her or met her on the road.'

'Stella went to see Joe?'

Tilly nodded. 'I told her she was mad.'

Luke straightened and scowled. 'Suicidal. How long ago?'

'A good half hour. I'm trying not to panic.'

'Why the hell did she do a fool thing like that?'

So far Tilly had never noticed any bitterness in Luke for all he'd gone through. But since seeing Joe it appeared he had gained some. He must be really hurting.

'She said it was for Alice.'

Her mind was torn between Ma still missing and Luke's obvious pain. She jammed her hands into her jeans pockets and focused on this man dealing with his own private torture.

'How was Joe?'

'Cold and arrogant.'

Tilly gasped. 'About Alice?'

He nodded and his mouth thinned. 'Got it all on tape though.'

'He confessed?' she whispered, stunned.

'Even boasted about it.'

Speechless, Tilly shook her head. The conceit!

Luke's gaze softened over her into such a look of agonising heartbreak, it took her breath away. How to help him? Ease his circumstances? Right now, she doubted anyone could but she would be here for him. Always.

In that moment, when Luke looked so desolate, her heart tumbled over with deep compassion. She ached to slide her arms around him and crush him tight in a comforting hug. Hold his blue-eyed gaze, run her palms over that sexy stubble, her fingers around those gorgeous available lips and press hers firm and soft against him. Shaken by her thoughts, she realised his importance in her life and how far her feelings for him had changed and grown.

Through her steamy trance, she heard Luke's mellow drawl jolt her back to reality. 'Stella's back.'

'Oh my God.'

Tilly didn't notice if Luke went into the cottage or back down to the machinery shed. Her attention focused on her mother. She swung around and strode toward the ute pulling up before the farmhouse fence.

'You said thirty minutes!' Tilly challenged as her Ma eased from the vehicle. She eyed her from head to boots. Slightly flushed and ruffled she noted in relief but not injured.

'Took longer than I expected.'

'What happened?'

'Gave him a piece of my mind and a bit more besides.'

Indoors, Tilly set the kettle to boil on the stove, knowing her mother would appreciate a strong sweet brew after her encounter. With a frustrated sigh, she muttered, 'That horrid man deserves more than a lashing from your sharp tongue.'

'He won't give us any more trouble.'

Tilly scoffed. 'The only way that's going to happen is when that worthless human being is given a dose of his own medicine. If I thought it was worthwhile, I'd go on over there and do it myself.'

'Don't worry, dear, that won't be necessary. I already did.'

Tilly spun around and scoffed, 'Ma! Don't joke.'

'I'm not.'

'What exactly have you done?' Tilly went cold until she had an answer.

'Didn't need to do a thing. Old bugger did it to himself.' She lowered herself slowly onto a kitchen chair. 'Course my rifle was pointed at him so he had no choice. Trust me, dear, he knows exactly what it's like now to be facing the wrong end of the gun himself.'

'Joe shot himself?'

Stella nodded. 'In the leg. Farm accidents happen.'

Utter silence fell between them while a stunned Tilly stared at her mother as she calmly folded her hands on the table and waited for her tea.

'You're serious!'

'He was bleeding out some but I passed Sergeant John on the way home. He'll be there now so I imagine the ambulance won't be far behind.'

'What if they find out it wasn't an accident? Joe will squeal.'

'Won't matter. No proof. Besides, after all he's done now, who'll believe him? He used his own rifle. I said my piece first for Alice but he won't be walking for a while. A bullet at close range sure messes up a leg.' Stella shook her head, calm and impressed.

Tilly couldn't believe this was her mother talking. 'If Sergeant John gets suspicious and comes asking questions, I'll have to tell him you were over there.'

Stella shrugged. 'I'll say I left before it happened.'

'I hope they trust your word then otherwise

you'll end up in prison.'

'Won't matter.'

Tilly studied her mother's composure and air of resignation, sensing all was not right here. 'Why not?'

'No one lives forever.'

Tilly chuckled to try and lighten the mood. 'You're not even seventy and as tough as a Mallee bull.' Ma used to be stronger. Privately, Tilly knew she was failing, sensed there was more coming and feared what she might be about to hear.

Stella's shoulders drooped and she heaved a long weary sigh. 'I'm not actually,' she said quietly.

'What do you mean?'

Her mother snapped, 'Go shut off that damn hissing kettle and we can talk.'

Still confused over what her mother had done and what was happening here, Tilly brought the tea tray to the table along with some fresh buttered scones. She poured their cups as Ma started talking.

'The other day when I went into town shopping I saw Dr. Singh again. Got the results of some tests a week ago.'

'What tests?' Tilly's shoulders sank with premonition. 'Dr. Singh didn't say anything to me the other day.'

'I told him not to tell you. You've been through hell in recent years and I didn't want you worrying extra about me. I said I'd talk to you. In my own time.'

The news wasn't good. After her mother had

explained, Tilly grew sick in the stomach and grabbed Stella's work-worn hands to hold in her own. 'There must be some treatment. Something they can do.'

Stella shook her head. 'No, dear. It's secondary. I'm sorry to be leaving you alone. I'm more worried about you than me.'

'Well that's just typical,' Tilly remarked, swiping away the tears escaping down her cheeks. She took a moment then asked, 'That why you bailed up Joe?'

Stella nodded. 'Nothing to lose.' She paused. 'The farm's on a long-term lease. Give you a decent income with your teaching. The agricultural company has already offered to buy our property so I know they're open to negotiations and would buy you out in a heartbeat. If that's what you want. Either way, this place is yours, my dear.' She paused. 'I just want to live out my life here. I don't want tears now but I have my heart set on one of those celebration of life services before I go.'

That wish reined in Tilly with wide-eyed attention. 'What!'

'I want to hear all the wonderful things people say at a memorial service about you after you're gone. No good missing out when you're already dead and in your coffin. A body never gets to hear it. Such a waste.'

Tilly gasped with a touch of admiration. 'Ma, I can't believe you want to do that!'

'I can and I will. Pastor is going to arrange it. He's putting an announcement in the church newsletter and local paper. Let everyone know

130

and have it as part of our normal Sunday service.'

'You've already spoken to him?'

'Not as crazy as it sounds, dear. Makes sense to me.' Stella finished her tea and slowly rose. 'I need to lie down for a bit. It's been a busy day.'

She hugged Tilly tight before taking herself off to her room, leaving a stunned already-grieving daughter standing in the middle of the kitchen. Tilly simply could not wrap her head around what her Ma had just shared.

Refusing to accept it and the impossible thought that sooner rather than later apparently. Ma would no longer be living in this house, she wearily forced her feet to move and headed for the only person she wanted to see.

* * *

Luke had been switched onto Tilly Schroder's every mood pretty much since he was a lovesick teenager. For him anyway, nothing had changed except now he was a lovesick adult. His heart raced and his libido went through the roof just looking at her.

So, as he sat outside the cottage toward sunset, sipping on a rare beer, waiting for the country air and nature to bring him peace from his churning mind since visiting Joe, he spotted Tilly's mood by the way she only sauntered toward him from the farmhouse. Reflective. Not her usual jaunty step.

That long bedroom hair was being lifted off her back and shoulders by the frisky evening

131

breeze that had sprung up. She was stunning, the woman of his dreams. If that was the only way he could have her, he never wanted to wake up.

He raised his stubbie as he approached. 'Can I offer you one?'

She frowned. 'Must have been bad with Joe. You don't drink.'

'Tonight's an exception.'

'Then I'll join you.'

He returned from indoors with another cold one for his favourite guest and another chair.

'Thanks,' she accepted the drink and dragged her chair closer to his.

She sat quiet awhile and sipped her drink.

'What's up?'

When Tilly told him what Stella did to Joe, he spluttered on his beer. 'The hell she did! Now that's my kind of woman.'

'Sergeant John was on his way as she drove home.'

'I should scoot over there to take John my phone recording.'

Tilly frowned. 'Can't it wait till morning? He'll have his hands full at the moment.

'It's a confession, Tilly,' he pointed out.

'I know. Well done you for thinking on your feet.'

'He needs to pay for what he did. Murder is committed where the act of causing death is done with reckless indifference to human life.'

Tilly raised her shapely eyebrows. 'Did you memorise that?'

He nodded. 'Googled it.'

She grinned and teased, 'Cover all your bases,

Hunter, don't you?'

When she used his surname, it stung. Who was he? Apparently he wasn't a Hunter. Alice didn't travel far. Had to be someone local.

When Tilly next spoke softly, glancing at him in appeal, she looked at him with such sadness his own troubled thoughts scattered at the words that issued quietly from that lovable mouth.

'Ma has incurable cancer.'

Because she broke down with such force, he knew she had been holding it in. They rose together and he wrapped his big arms so tight around her she pretty much disappeared. He felt her shaking and sobbing. He kissed the top of her head beneath his chin, murmured useless words and caressed her back until her personal storm eased.

The moment's intimacy took a subtle shift as they drew ever so slightly apart, their faces achingly close. Her eyes pleaded and her mouth beckoned. He stole their first kiss with deliberate tenderness, wanting it to be memorable for her, his body knowing a rush of passion that Tilly returned.

Later, sitting on his knee, her arms linked around his neck, he let her talk, listened to the words flow. Loved the curve of her mouth even more since their long and smoking hot first kiss. And sent up a silent prayer of thanks that just maybe she had a place in her heart for him.

Because Tilly's responsive body and kiss had let him know her feelings were real and thriving, he no longer suffered the thoughts he had when he first returned to Bingun that he was moving in on his dead brother's fiancé. He was confident they shared more than that now and their attraction could only deepen.

'Do you have any better news?' Tilly asked wryly.

Luke wavered whether to confide about his paternity until he learned more but he'd known this woman all his life and loved her for most of it.

Holding such strong feelings, he needed her to be the first to know. Because if she had second thoughts or pushed him away, he wanted to hear it straight. He didn't really expect a negative reaction but until he knew his real father's identity it felt like juggling emotional balls in the air.

So he ploughed ahead. 'I have news but it's more like unexpected.'

He started off slow, relating the information as easy as he knew how about the real reason behind why Christian's life ended too soon. Tilly sank into shock, wide-eyed with disbelief. She wrapped her arms around her waist, bent over and moaned. He let her take time to process the truth in the train wreck of circumstances that assaulted both their lives right now.

Eventually, barely above a whisper and slowly shaking her head, she said, 'Christian wasn't meant to die! Alice and another man! Joe's not your father!'

'Whoever my natural father is, I just hope he's a damn decent man.'

'If he's anything like you, he's bound to be.'

'He might not even want to know me.'

Tilly was adamant. 'Your mother would never

134

have connected with someone that wasn't honourable.'

'You're not bothered that I might potentially have a whole other family?'

When Tilly shook her head, that luscious mouth tipped into a wry grin and her creamy sun-lightened hair bounced softly about her face and shoulders.

She straightened and eased from his lap. 'Tell you what. I should go check on Ma. Come up to the house. She and Alice were best friends. She might know something.'

As they started walking, a soft warm hand slipped into his and their fingers entwined. He felt a wave of love and pride for this woman spread across his chest. A love he'd felt most of his life but kept hidden inside. Even now, feeling as he did, he wasn't sure how he could put it into words. Loaded with the extra burdens of dealing as they all were with other traumas.

Joe deliberately killed his mother.

Joe Hunter wasn't his father.

Stella was dying.

What next?

Life was throwing them a hell of a lot of curve balls these days but, together with this woman, they would handle whatever was thrown their way. With Tilly Schroder by his side, the promise of her love lent him courage. They would be around for each other.

They were both dealing with hell in their lives at the moment. When the black times passed, they would emerge stronger. United.

★ ★ ★

A pair of wise old eyes watched the two young people from a farmhouse window. Their grateful owner sighed and smiled with contentment. 'Thank you, Lord,' she whispered.

10

'Ma, you're awake. You okay?' Tilly asked as she and Luke stepped inside.

'Just needed a rest. Lucas,' she greeted. 'Suppose my daughter's told you what I did to Joe.'

'I admire your restraint,' he drawled wryly.

Stella laid a hand on his arm. 'I know he's your family, Lucas, and it wasn't my place but I did it for your mother. Alice was like a sister to me.'

'I understand. I had trouble keeping my hands off him as well.'

'This crime is affecting so many people.' Stella sighed and glanced at the clock. 'I passed John's police car heading in Joe's direction as I came home. He should be arrested by now and out of harm's way.'

'It's been on my mind to phone Karen Bennett,' Tilly said. 'She'll have more information and I'd like to know how Chloe's doing. Just a quick call. Their family will be in chaos, too.'

'She would appreciate that, dear.'

Five minutes later Tilly returned with news. 'Karen said Chloe's understandably traumatized but seems to feel better when she talks about it. They have to continually reassure her Joe is in gaol and never getting out to hurt anyone again. But for the moment, she's doing okay. The Bennetts are a close family.

'Karen said Chloe was overcome in the police station when the family all went in together so she could give a statement. I suggested Karen keep her home until she was really ready to go back to school. For now, I can set up work she can do online and call in on them as needed.' Tilly turned to Luke. 'Karen said Joe was taken by ambulance to Horsham hospital and he'll be undergoing an operation on his leg. When he's recovered enough he'll be released, questioned and then taken into custody, possibly down to Melbourne.' She shrugged. 'Anyone have an appetite?'

Luke nodded. 'I could handle some grub. Can I help?'

'I have some fillet steaks in the fridge if you don't mind tossing them on the barbeque. I'll do some sliced potatoes and onions to grill as well.'

'Sure.'

Stella retired to her recliner by the fire in the lounge while Luke and Tilly worked alongside each other in the kitchen. Tilly made a tossed salad. Half an hour later they sat around the table eating and drinking, mulling through the day's developments. It had been a long and memorable one in so many different ways for them all.

'Lucas,' Stella hesitated, 'I'm not feeling much peace on behalf of your mother. I know it's probably rude of me to ask but can I hear what Joe said on that recording?'

Luke glanced between the women. 'You sure?'

Tilly shook her head but Stella shrugged. 'Sometimes facing things helps us deal with them.'

After Luke warned the women Joe's language

was blunt and cruel, Stella and Tilly listened in subdued awe to the earlier conversation over at the Hunter farm.

When it reached the part where Joe insulted his wife with offensive language, Stella interrupted with an explosive, 'She. Was. Not! Alice Hunter was a good Christian woman. Driven to the edge,' she said fiercely.

'Stella, I'm sorry.' Luke stopped the recording.

She took a deep breath to steady her shaking anger. 'It's all right. You have the proof you need. That's what's important. I had no idea he was so heartless.' Her brow wrinkled in emotional pain. 'Poor Alice,' she whispered, distressed, growing quiet and pale.

'Ma,' Tilly reached out, 'you feeling worse?'

'No! Don't fuss just yet. I'll be worse soon enough. I needed to know.'

'Of course.' Tilly rubbed her arms, rose to add another log to the fire and backed up against it. 'It's hard to hear all this. What staggers me is how a person turns so evil.'

Stella willingly started talking, reminiscing. She seemed to need it.

'I knew Joe Hunter's parents. They were battlers with a big family and always did it tough. Their small rundown property was established when Joe's father, Ted Hunter, took up a soldier settlement block after the Second World War. Originally it was a dairy farm then he added some cropping. He was well known in the district for having returned angry and become a bully, greatly affected by his war service and the horrors he must have seen. These days a

139

returned soldier might be given counselling and support.

'Ted was abusive to his wife, a hard man who thrashed his children, including Joe, the youngest of the ten kids. Everyone knew but in those days you said nothing. Joe's parents Ted and Maisie are long gone and all their kids left Bingun and scattered. Split as soon as they could. Some of them, especially the boys, while they were still teenagers. Far as I know, according to Alice one time, all family links are broken. Joe just stayed on and claimed the farm.'

Stella sighed. 'So young Joe surely learned poor behaviour from his father and just carried on in his own family. That it was okay to mistreat a woman. At first I think Alice tried to please him, calm him down, make excuses for his behaviour. But then it grew harder. You could see it in her face. Life was surely a struggle for her as you know, Lucas.'

'Why did Alice stay with Joe in such a hard loveless marriage? Did she ever say?' Tilly appealed to her mother and shared an expressive glance with Luke.

His hopeful blue eyes settled on Stella and Tilly suspected he craved answers.

Stella took a moment then said to Luke, 'I knew your mother all her life. We were at school around the same time. She was a few years younger than me but we became friends later before we married. I used to cycle in every day from my parents' farm on the other side of town to work in Picketts Hardware. I managed the garden nursery and supplies section. Loved it.

140

Knew Carl through church, of course, and him coming into the store regular for years.

'Alice Dawson, as she was back then,' Stella smiled gently, 'became my best friend. Her parents were George and Anna. He worked on the railways. Alice became a nurse at the local bush nursing hospital. Of course that's closed now but we have our new medical centre. She did district nursing, too. That's how she met Joe. His father, Ted, had died and his mother Maisie was ill. By then Joe was working the farm alone and his mother lived out there, too.

'As you know, Tilly, your Schroder ancestors were early German farming immigrants who selected land. In the late 1940s, Ted Hunter moved onto their small government soldier settlement block and that's when the Hunters and Schroders became farming neighbours. So when Alice and I married later, we were delighted to live so close.

'Apparently the abuse started before you were born, Lucas. But later when you came along Joe claimed Alice should be giving Christian more attention, that she was wasting too much time on her youngest child. The bad treatment grew worse.'

Tilly cast a quick side glance to Luke who she knew would reveal his truth when he was ready.

'I'm sorry, Lucas. I know Alice loved both of you boys equally. Just Joe's delusions, I imagine.'

'Interesting recollection, Stella,' Luke said uncomfortably, 'because today Joe claimed I'm not his son.'

Stella gasped, her body still and rigid. 'He did?'

141

'I was so shocked at first thinking he was disowning me like he usually does. Then I saw the gleam of satisfaction in his eyes and understood what he had been actually saying all my life. He meant it. It's probably true. I was so mad at him I didn't challenge him on it or push further.' Luke paused. 'So I'm asking you straight out, Stella, if you know something. Is it true Joe Hunter's not my father?'

Tilly noticed her mother blanch and fidget. She knew something!

Stella took a moment to compose herself again then bravely addressed Luke. 'I've known all these years but your mother swore me to secrecy not to say anything about the visits. In the circumstances, with all your family truths coming to light and my health not being so good, it's time to break my promise.' She glanced toward the ceiling. 'I trust Alice will forgive me. I'll be seeing her soon anyway so I'll apologise to her myself.'

Tilly caught her breath. Her mother had always been open and honest to the point of being blunt so she wasn't about to change now. All the same it was difficult hearing the mortal reality of her dearest flesh and blood being voiced.

'All I know, Lucas,' Stella continued, 'is that one night when it got real bad, your mother told me she feared for her life and Christian who was only a toddler at the time so she went across the paddock to their nearest neighbour on the back end of the property for protection. Apparently Joe was drunk and passed out so she took the opportunity to leave while she could. She said she didn't think about where to go just where it was close and safe.'

Luke frowned. 'The Meyer's place?'

Stella nodded, giving them a moment to drink in the import of that knowledge before she added, 'I know she relied on Dave many times. Maybe it was more than that. His parents had retired and moved into town. Dave lived alone on the farm. She always spoke fondly of him. To be honest, I don't know for sure. Alice never admitted a thing but it's entirely possible that he could be your father.'

She allowed her quiet assumption to settle in Luke's mind. Tilly watched him from across the short space between them in the room. His eyes had widened that the speculation could be even a remote possibility.

Everyone realised what this meant. Luke was possibly not Joe's son. Because Alice never left Bingun, it must be a local man. And the likelihood was pointing directly across town in Dave Meyer's direction.

With suspicion cast, it was impossible not to compare Luke and Dave. The similarities were more real than imagined. If you thought about it, the two men both had sandy hair, that quiet easy manner, although Luke had only settled into a more stable person over time and with life's experience in recent years.

What a predicament!

Did Dave Meyer know?

Tilly wondered if Luke would approach him and put the challenging question. If Dave wasn't his father, that conversation could end up in red-faced embarrassment.

And how ironic that Joe Hunter, outwardly notorious for being an old fool, was way more sinister than anyone imagined. The deliberate twisted setup and reality now was that Dave Meyer was probably with his son Lucas while his lover Alice was being murdered by her husband.

'Stella,' Luke eventually said, sitting forward in his chair, staring at the floor, hands folded on his knees, 'thank you for sharing and breaking a promise. I appreciate your honesty.' He rose, hands on hips and surveyed the women in turn, a combination of confusion and disbelief etched in his face. 'Thank you for your hospitality. I'll head back to the cottage. Got some thinking to do.'

Tilly ached to follow but his withdrawn gaze held her back. 'Take care,' she folded her arms. 'We're always here for you.'

'I know it. Night,' he mumbled and abruptly left.

Ma went straight to bed after Luke walked out, leaving Tilly with too many thoughts and feelings drawing her toward him. Out there alone, too. She didn't even have Isla for comfort anymore which only engulfed her in fresh sadness. As if there wasn't enough of that stuff around at the moment.

What an exhausting Monday. How was she supposed to front up to school tomorrow after everything that had happened in the last ten hours? Chloe Bennett sure wouldn't attend and Tilly would only be there in body. Her mind was with the man she was growing to love and the mother she already did.

Well Tilly Schroder, she took herself in hand, it's the last week before holidays. Put on the same brave face you always do, forget about yourself while you're with your kids and do your job.

All the same, right now after she snapped off all the farmhouse lights and stood in the dark, she didn't resist one last lingering look out toward the cottage.

No lights over there either. Was Luke sitting in the dark, too, or already asleep? She doubted it. An image of that tall muscled man stretched out possibly half naked in bed did her head in and caused a wave of heat through her body. Did he want to be alone or could he use a friend?

Feeling nervous and bold at the same time, she pushed open the screen door, paused on the veranda, then took the steps down and strolled across the yard. Heart pounding, she tapped on the closed cottage door. No sound or movement or light going on.

'Luke?' Nothing. If he was inside, he would have responded by now.

She hadn't thought to bring a torch but she found her way in the half moonlight down to the machinery shed. The Monaro was gone! With its throaty engine, how had she not heard it leave? He must have cruised out real slow. Clearly he needed space or maybe he had taken his phone recording into the Bingun police station.

Either way, Tilly's disappointment was epic. 'Well, watch out Luke Hunter,' she muttered, 'I'm a boomerang. I'm coming back.' Pushing out a heavy sigh, she headed back to the house.

Early next morning just before daybreak, Tilly was roused from sleep by the sound of running water from down the hall. Always cautious these days watching out for her mother, she scrambled from bed, padding barefoot in her silky pyjamas and pushed the bathroom door ajar.

'Ma, do you need my help?'

She reeled back in surprise to see a lean athletic body standing in the middle of the steamed up room.

'Luke! Sorry.' Awkward. She half turned to leave.

'Can't say I am,' he drawled, raising arched brows, grinning, his blue eyes doing a visual strip search from her tousled hair, meeting her gaze and slowing down over the shoestring straps and half exposed breasts. Then moving lower over her hips and shapely legs all the way to her toes and back up again.

'Cheeky,' she tossed out, wide-eyed.

Tilly could barely breathe at the vision of a naked Luke, except for the small and highly inadequate towel sitting dangerously low on his hips. Impressive. Of course that could be a result of her man drought. Or the memory of their first sizzling unforgettable kiss.

They locked gazes as he stepped closer, Tilly spellbound, clamped to the cold tiles under her feet. He slid a damp bare arm around her waist so that their willing bodies melted together.

Her body fizzed with anticipation as his head dipped and his luscious full mouth clung soft and warm to hers. The kiss was slow and

146

confident and lifted her desire levels off the chart.

When it ended, he kissed the tip of her nose and the dip between her neck and shoulder before pulling back to murmur, 'Stella might be scandalised.'

Tilly chuckled. 'She's broadminded. You're early.'

As she leaned against the door, watching and drooling, her body still humming from that kiss, Luke stepped back, grabbed a denim shirt and shrugged it on.

'The grain merchant phoned last night. I start driving today. Taking a load of malt barley down to a Melbourne brewery. Then sounds like tomorrow I'll be trucking wheat down the coast to Portland for shipping out.'

Her only thought was how she would miss him.

'I'm on the clock now,' he teased and started to loosen the towel.

Tilly held up her hands. 'Another time.'

'Definitely.'

Reluctantly, she closed the door again and virtually floated back to her room. Well, that sure took her mind off her problems.

11

Luke checked all his truck mirrors, crunched into gear and slowly pulled away from the grain bunker. His mind was still being drawn back to the image of a sleepy blonde in clingy pyjamas that had outlined every enticing dip and curve on her body.

Man it was getting harder to resist such a country angel. It had been a long time between women. He was no saint but Tilly was special and he needed the moment to be right.

It was good to be working again, feeling useful. It meant being away from Bingun but sounded like most of his driving would be day jobs with only an occasional long haul. By day's end he knew he'd be hankering to get back home. For Bingun would always be his home base and he now had the strongest reason to stay. Not just any woman but the sweet temptation who owned his heart.

Despite his family as he once knew it splintering into pieces, its previous truths broken, he clung to memories. He would always cherish the good woman who was his mother and the half-brother he wished was still around. He certainly wouldn't miss the man who he'd always known as his father and never wanted to clap eyes on the brutal S.O.B. again.

Before leaving town, Luke figured hauling on the road would be valuable time to think. Hours later, halfway to his city destination on the A8, he was beginning to realise maybe it was too much time.

He had replayed the Dave Meyer quandary a hundred times already. Wasn't even definite the guy was his father but if it turned out that way, he would be damn proud. Dave was a bloke everyone respected but Luke could look like the biggest idiot if he reached out and made contact only to have his paternity disproved.

If Dave was his father, he would never deny it. He was too honest. But how would he take the forced prospect of a difficult conversation?

And why had his mother never told him he was another man's son? He guessed it had a lot to do with shame. An admission of disloyalty to her husband would not have been easy for a Christian woman who broke her marriage vows. All the same, Luke felt disappointed not to know. He would have preferred to hear it from Alice and the regret sat heavy on his shoulders.

After driving a few more miles, it hit him that maybe his mother was afraid Luke would reject her! Or leave. As if. He only wished she had at least given him a break and taken him into her confidence while she was still alive.

It occurred to him that he would be seeing Dave Meyer around town but he'd handle that meeting when the time came. So far, he had only seen him from a distance in the main street, before the seed was planted that there could be more between them than he knew.

Or there could be nothing and he would need to keep searching.

Tilly missed Luke during the week while he was away driving every day. After the first invitation, he had settled into the routine of strolling up to the farmhouse when he returned for dinner with them.

Dusty and tired, he usually showered before everyone sat around the kitchen table and shared their day. What warmed her heart and made her soul sing was when Luke first walked in and smiled, then kissed her. In front of Ma. Except Stella was either watching television or pretending to read but really she was mostly dozing by the fire, only lit now in the evenings as the October days grew milder.

Once school was out, Tilly was officially free for a fortnight. The Bennetts were heading down to the coast so she hoped the family holiday and change of scenery would help Chloe heal, although the process would no doubt be gradual and the memories with her for life.

Despite Luke's visible affection, there was an understandable air of distraction about him that was impossible to miss. Tilly got it, that he sometimes preferred to wander down to the machinery shed and tinker with Nev's Monaro, so she stepped back while he was coming to terms with his new family situation. His mother and brother were dead, both at the hands of the man who was in hospital before cooling his tough old heels in custody awaiting trial for murder.

Although Luke wasn't physically around much he was certainly in her thoughts. Tilly found it hard seeing him walk off alone each night back to the cottage. She longed to go with him. A night would come when she was confident he would not let her leave.

So she would wait. Impatiently. And it would be all the more special for the unspoken promise revealed from Luke's steady hooded gazes. Oh, she planned to learn every inch of that gorgeous body. Real slow.

Tilly's joy in her new romance was overshadowed by troubled thoughts for her mother. She noticed that Stella was openly tending to rely on a walking stick for support. It crushed her daughter to watch her Ma weaken which also meant she was unable to do little gardening these days, sad and confronting for a woman who had been unceasingly active her whole life. Then again, Tilly thought, trying to stay hopeful, maybe it was just because she was home around the farmhouse and on the property all the time in the school holidays that she noticed more than usual.

Stella's previous bravado had obviously been a front and she now seemed to have accepted the truth of her illness and silently conceded to her declining health. No words were necessary. Tilly noted the winces of pain and discomfort but determined to at least stay outwardly cheerful and positive.

So under Stella's keen-eyed supervision, Tilly took on the responsibility for her mother's stunning productive garden.

While she dug over the freshly composted soil and marked lines to sow more vegetable seeds one morning with the mid-spring sun beating down, her mother sat in a cane chair nearby, her weathered face shaded by her large brimmed garden hat.

'I'm so pleased I'm passing from this life in spring,' Stella commented. 'The garden is looking so magnificent it would be a shame to miss. Plenty of flowers for my service next Sunday.'

Tilly swallowed hard to staunch tears when her mother made such frank candid remarks lately. And they were happening much more often. So she just nodded and smiled.

Ma was right though. So much new growth was bursting into creation. Some paddocks in the countryside were already a sweep of yellow with flowering canola. Others were a vast swathe of tall green wheat or barley stalks that drifted before the fickle spring breezes, their feathery heads filling with grain.

The budding orchard and floral farmhouse garden had become a humming haven of nectar for the bees. The night sky was perhaps her favourite view, its usual clear realm studded with stars.

Tilly loved it all, this country life with space, fresh air and open roads. It was all too cruelly beautiful and vibrant at the moment when another living soul was being slowly stolen away from her.

Just days ago, her mother had taken an alarming turn. A token signal that all was not well, as if they needed to be reminded. Stella had collapsed in the house, similar to the one in the garden when Luke first arrived and came to help.

Tilly phoned Dr Singh at the medical centre and he immediately drove out to the farm. After a thorough check, the doctor suggested Ma take more bed rest. Of course the unflagging woman muttered her objections, saying she would have plenty of time to rest soon enough. In an exchanged look of resignation, Dr Singh raised amused eyebrows and Tilly just shook her head.

At this stage, Stella must be allowed to cope with her failing health in her own way.

Tilly fought annoyance and compassion on behalf of her mother and grieved in private from the extra strain. Little things seemed larger. Ma's gardening cargoes with their umpteen pockets, usually full of tools, seed packets and secateurs now hung limply on a peg in the utility room.

So Tilly was surprised one morning when Ma said from her cane chair on the sunny north veranda while they sipped hot tea and crunched Anzac biscuits, 'It's a glorious day. I might take the ute for a drive.'

'You feel strong enough?'

'I'll be fine.'

'That's not what I asked.'

'I have an errand to run.'

'Is it urgent?'

Stella shrugged. 'Depends on your definition.'

'Wherever you need to go I can take you.'

Stella reached out and placed her thin brown hand over her daughter's. 'One last time, dear. I'll take this,' she waved her mobile in the air.

'What if you're not well enough to use it?'

'Possible but I'm not quite ready to go yet. I'm looking forward to my celebration of life service.

I can't miss that,' she grinned.

Tilly didn't bother to ask where she was going. Stella wouldn't tell her anyway. A short time later, as her mother slowly drove away from the farmhouse and down the eucalyptus drive to the main road, Tilly just sighed and prayed.

And gave silent thanks when she returned more than an hour later.

★ ★ ★

On the Saturday of the last weekend before school resumed and the day before the significant Sunday chosen for Stella's celebration of life service, Tilly and her mother spent a full day in town.

In the morning early at Ma's command, Tilly raided the farm garden, cutting every long stemmed flower and bunches of greenery, including an armful of wheat from the closest paddock to the house.

In town at their church, the guild ladies began to arrive and together they worked harmoniously creating fabulous floral displays for tomorrow's special service. Everyone knew about it but the atmosphere was made easier because sitting in the empty front pew watching them work, Stella openly chatted, tossed out instructions, and even encouraged the ladies to consider such an occasion themselves.

For lunch, Tilly managed to walk her mother across the street to Irma's cafe where Stella could only manage a small bowl of soup but Tilly chose the menu specialty of crispy battered fish and salad. They lingered over a shared pot of tea until it was time to meet their Pastor at the manse.

Whereas the morning had actually been fun and the results of their efforts a number of huge vases of stunning arrangements, Tilly wasn't looking forward to the more serious aspect of her mother's service. But she politely endured while Pastor and Stella chatted.

Thinking ahead, she had already decided and informed the school Principal that she would not return to teaching and needed indefinite family leave to stay on the farm.

As the day progressed, Tilly's emotional stamina grew shaky. She felt drained but kept pushing through for her mother's sake. Yet Stella seemed energised, even inspired, and ready for tomorrow's experience. Although feeling herself falling to pieces, Tilly held it together, smiling through their usual meal and conversation with Luke that evening, almost grateful when he returned to the cottage.

But as soon as Stella settled for the night, Tilly stayed with her, as was her habit these days, until her breathing grew steady.

Then she quietly rose, stopped in the bathroom to freshen up, free her hair from its pony tail band and brushed it long and slow. She examined her reflection in the mirror. Denim shorts, shapely enough brown legs and a cotton gypsy blouse suitably unbuttoned halfway down, not enough to be brazen but just enough to display an enticing amount of cleavage. She figured the less she wore the less there would be for Luke to take off.

Made sense.

Tilly planted her hands on her hips, half turned both ways and whispered, 'You'll pass.'

With a jaunty step, she walked over to the cottage. A light shone out from inside so when she peered through the window, she moaned. Luke was stretched out sitting on the bed, top half naked and promising. Bottom half covered in hip hugging jeans. Feet bare. Damn.

She didn't bother to knock and leaned back against the door after she closed it. 'Tell me to leave if you want.'

His mouth didn't quite make it into a smile and he held out an arm of beckoning encouragement. Tilly swaggered across the small room and took it, sliding onto the single bed beside him.

Still sitting up, he reached an arm around behind her and drew her close. 'To what do I owe the pleasure?'

'Ma's service tomorrow is getting to me.' Tilly halted, shocked to feel herself choking up, finally expressing the feelings that had been building for weeks. 'I just need someone to talk to,' her voice cracked.

'Glad you came,' he murmured. 'I'm always here for you.'

And then just when she thought she had it all planned and under control — the past week's highs and lows, today's preparations and planning for the tomorrow's service — the heart-warming sound of Luke's deep voice tipped her over the edge. Her emotions broke. Bringing tears. Lots of them. Rolling over her cheeks like steady rain.

'She's so excited about the service,' Tilly sobbed, 'really looking forward to it. You know she's going to get up and speak? How will she stand?' she sniffed, swiping at her wet face. 'It feels like her funeral already but she's still here. And over a week ago, she jumped in the ute and disappeared for over an hour. I was worried sick.'

Luke just listened, squeezed her tighter, kissed the top of her head and drawled softly, 'Tilly, honey, everything happens in its own time. Just let it. Go with the flow. It's what Stella wants.'

'You're right, damn it. How did you get to be so smart?' she muttered, her torrent of emotions subsiding.

He shrugged and chuckled. 'Took a while. Like, years.'

It had been so long since there was someone, anyone, with whom she was able to share. Once, she thought Christian would be that person but that was the past. Now she had this awesome man who had drifted back into her life and a promising new future seemed possible. Her heart was no longer empty but full again. And she knew with every bit of love she possessed, it belonged to him.

But first and foremost, Luke had become her friend, a confidante, and for tonight that was all she needed. So now, thinking breathtaking sex would fix all her problems, her plans seemed tacky. Wasn't going to happen. She knew the fantastic prospect would still take place but it wouldn't be rushed. She was thinking long slow lovemaking that occurred naturally when it was meant to.

'Sorry, didn't mean this to be all about me,' she snuffled, slowly pulling herself together. 'How are you feeling about . . . everything?'

'You mean Dave?'

She nodded.

'Can't help thinking how much I look like the guy actually. He's a good man, community minded. A bloke to admire and respect. The proverbial gentle giant. If it turns out to be him, I'd find it hard to lay blame. Mum sought him out for a genuine reason and I have to think was it such a bad thing they found love together?' He gave a soft laugh. 'And you know what? Dave has always called me *son*. Like when Chris and I would go over and work for him. *How you doing, son?* I thought he was just being friendly. That was his way. And maybe it was. But what if all this time he's known? And if he has, did my mother tell him or did he work it out for himself?'

Tilly turned into Luke and snuggled against him, wrapped her arms around all that amazing bare skin for comfort. He felt warm and so good.

'Damn,' he cursed, his mind still on Dave. 'If he knew, I would have liked him to say something. After Mum died maybe, you know? So what happens now? Do I wait?'

'Won't be a perfect time however it happens,' Tilly said.

'That's what I'm thinking. I can't believe my gentle mother had the courage to love another man and yet still stay with Joe in our lousy home.'

Tilly's heart filled with understanding for Luke. He clearly needed more time to face his issue, somehow find a way to meet with Dave and reassess his identity. He could potentially have a whole different family life situation with a father in the picture. This whole Dave thing was *big*.

They talked a while longer until it grew late.

'I should be getting back to Ma. Don't like leaving her alone too long.'

Tilly reluctantly unwound herself from Luke and slid from the bed. He followed and bailed her up against the door before she left. His kisses were hypnotic and stirred her body, his hands reverently roaming and caressing with her blessing.

'Night, beautiful.' He drew away and kissed the tip of her nose.

'One night you won't want to get rid of me,' she whispered against his mouth.

He groaned and chuckled. 'I don't already.'

'For so long I didn't believe I would ever find someone else.' Unspoken heartache lay behind her words. What could have been.

'I want to be everything you need.'

'You already are.' She kissed him gently one last time. 'My heart's yours. I belong to you.'

Parting made Tilly's entire body ache with unanswered longing. Soon, she knew. Soon. And it was going to be so worth the wait. Despite all the pain going on around them right now, she found herself smiling with promised pleasure, her mind filled with the deepest anticipation as she walked back to the farmhouse.

There was only one other small obstacle still to lick that Luke didn't know about. But not while their current problems were in play.

12

Stella was up and half dressed — far too early — when Tilly rose next morning.

She stood in her mother's bedroom doorway, arms crossed, shaking her head. 'You're keen, Ma. Are you going into town now to sit in the front pew or wait in the vestibule to greet the congregation as they arrive?' she teased.

'Takes me longer these days,' Stella grumbled with good humour. 'I'll need you to help me get my hair under control and maybe use just a little makeup.'

'Sure, but put on your dressing gown. Breakfast first. You need to keep up your strength.'

Later, Tilly gently groomed her mother's wild hair into submission with softer waves and the touch of makeup she requested, leaving Stella to dress while she showered and did the same.

When Stella shuffled into the kitchen where Tilly waited, her daughter gasped. 'Ma, you look gorgeous!'

Clearly this morning's celebration service held deep meaning and importance for her courageous mother. To say goodbye.

Usually clad in an old denim shirt and gardening cargoes with Crocs or rubber boots on her feet, today her thin body was smartly and softly clothed in a simple fitted red dress. With a black and gold fringed shawl draped around her shoulders, her feet pushed into a pair of low heeled comfortable shoes.

'Thank you, dear. I want to look better than I feel. Not just show up. *Arrive*, as they say!'

'Ma, you're priceless.' Tilly chuckled and they hugged.

Stella squeezed her tight. 'My precious only child.'

'I'm going to miss you so much,' Tilly whispered, still clinging to the woman so dear to her heart.

'Of course you will but don't grieve too long,' she murmured close to her ear. 'Move on and make every moment count. You of all people know how fragile life can be. I can tell you that a sense of freedom comes with age. Growing older isn't all bad. Although some days it feels like it.'

When mother and daughter pulled apart, Stella said, 'Blue suits you and I've always loved that dress.'

'I know. That's why I wore it. This is your day after all. I haven't seen your outfit before. Is that the *errand* you had to do last week when you went off in the ute?'

'No, dear.' She paused in reflection. 'This was the ensemble I wore for our last anniversary dinner with Carl before he died.'

In that moment, Tilly understood that her father would be with them today. Her mother's sentimental gesture to him. On the drive into Bingun, Stella grew silent and thoughtful but seemed content.

At the church, Tilly asked, 'Can you manage?'

Looking graceful but frail, Stella said, 'Yes but

161

I'll need my walking stick in one hand and my other arm looped through yours.'

'Done.'

Vehicles were parked on both sides of the street, the overflowing carpark already full. It seemed the whole district had turned out and that by itself made Tilly so proud of her mother. An honourable tribute.

As they steadily walked the pathway to the front porch, Luke was waiting. Sometimes he needed to work away on weekends so Tilly was grateful for his presence this morning. She wondered if he may even have asked to be free today. Knowing him as she did now it was something he might have deliberately arranged.

After their time together last night, she sensed a closer special bond between them. It was the first time she had ever seen him in a suit, wouldn't have believed he owned one living humbly as he had been doing for years.

The man was ruggedly handsome and no mistake. His sandy hair was neatly combed although that errant wave escaped to dip across his forehead as usual, she noted and smiled. He responded with a polite kiss on the cheek for Tilly and a respectful nod to Stella, publicly sealing the significant place he now held in their family.

Then all three moved slowly down the aisle and sat together in the reserved front pew, Luke stepping aside for the women to take their seat before he slipped in beside Tilly. He sought her hand, squeezed it and linked his warm fingers through hers. She had been uncertain how she

162

would cope today but his reassuring gesture lent her emotional strength.

The usual Sunday worship began with rousing hymns in-between Bible readings and prayers, then Stella's celebration of life service was introduced instead of the normal sermon. Firstly Pastor delivered a comprehensive eulogy, no doubt compiled during previous visits and reviewed during his time with her mother yesterday.

Then followed a parade of community leaders, women of the CWA, the garden club and the church guild ladies, each with glowing words of thanks and praise for Stella Schroder's tireless volunteering work for local clubs with lighter moments and anecdotes about her forthright but utterly unselfish nature.

Toward the end of the service, Tilly's mother made shaky progress as she steadily walked the few close steps to the front of the congregation, in her determination aided only by her walking stick.

Resting her folded hands on the small lectern for support, her often times aching back now just that little bit straighter, she launched into a brief reminiscence. Living her whole life in the small country town of Bingun, the blessing of her marriage to Carl and their decades of wonderful happy years together.

Tilly felt undeserving when her mother spoke with such warmth and love for her daughter Matilda May now devotedly serving their town by teaching the local children and her personal pride in the woman she had become.

Above all, interspersed with her mother's

sharp wry humour and bittersweet undertones as she remembered her dear lifetime friend Alice Hunter, Stella's attitude was one of uplifting gratitude.

Tilly loved her mother all the more for her courage in the face of delicate health to remain so positive with not a hint of self-pity. Anyone hearing her Ma speak this morning would leave this special service feeling inspired.

As her mother shakily resumed her seat beside Tilly, the congregation stood and applauded. An occasion the congregation and district people would no doubt fondly remember and talk about for years.

When Tilly and her mother walked back along the red carpet toward the open double doors at the other end leading to the porch and beckoning sunshine, she noticed Dave Meyer standing toward the rear of the church staring in their direction. For a moment, Tilly wasn't sure if it was in tribute to her mother or interest in the man who walked behind them.

Outside, the hum of friendly conversation resumed, people hugged and kissed, gathered in knots on the lawns chatting as they usually did after Sunday service.

Today, many also detained Stella in personal farewell. Some of her oldest and dearest friends including Irma from the cafe among them. People from other churches or those who might not normally attend. All shocked and saddened to learn of Stella's poor health.

Tilly wasn't at all surprised the Bennett family was absent. A daunted Chloe possibly preferring

164

to avoid crowds or public situations. It might be years before she worked through the trauma of having to relive her dreadful childhood experience.

Tilly hovered close to her weakening mother's side for safety. Luke had excused himself and disappeared to chat to farmers and townsfolk. People he would once have known and bravely making the effort to renew old friendships to those unaware that he was back in the district.

Tilly frowned as she watched him, afraid he might be excluded in some way because of his family background. Gossip had surely spread.

During one such roving glance, because both men were tall, she caught sight of Dave Meyer as he approached Luke. Interesting. She held her breath. Luke didn't appear too unduly shocked. The two men shook hands, Dave seemed to be doing most of the talking but only briefly, perhaps no more than a minute. Luke sank his hands into his trouser pockets, nodding and listening until they shook hands again and Dave strode away.

She had an urge to dash across the grass, grab Luke's arm and drag him aside to find out what was said. But Nev Reed, bless his big-hearted grease monkey soul, sidled up to Luke instead. No prizes for guessing what they would chat about.

A short time later, Tilly settled her exhausted mother in a comfortable chair in the hall with a cup of tea and plate of sandwiches. Just as she was leaving, anxious to find Luke, edging past people lining up for the usual morning tea and social gathering before all going their separate ways, he finally headed in her direction.

She raised her eyebrows in query, eager to hear what was happening.

He kissed her on the cheek — again, and in public — caught her hand and drawled, 'We're meeting out at his place this afternoon.' She opened her mouth but before she could speak, Luke added, 'Said he knew I was back in the district and wanted to discuss a work offer.'

'Really? Is that all?'

Luke shrugged. 'At least it's a one-on-one chance to open up a conversation.'

She nodded toward the hall. 'Coming in for a cuppa?'

He shook his head. 'Nev wants to check out the Monaro and discuss the work needed on it.'

'When will you eat?'

'Nev and Lorraine invited me to grab a bite at his place.'

Tilly chuckled. 'Then you'll be well fed.'

They reluctantly parted and, when her weary but contented mother was ready, Tilly drove her home for a well-earned rest.

13

While Luke and Nev waited for Lorraine to put the finishing touches to their roast lamb lunch, they removed their suit coats and ties, rolled up their sleeves and walked next door to the only garage in town where Luke had parked the Monaro.

Nev lifted the bonnet and the guys hung over the engine, getting down to some serious mechanical discussion.

'I noticed she was leaking water and overheating,' Luke said. 'Just needed to tighten a clamp yesterday. But the front end might need alignment. She's pulling to the left.'

'Can do that this arvo if you got time,' Nev suggested.

'Have to meet Dave Meyer for a while. He might have some harvest work for me soon. Maybe later on?'

'Sure. Bring her back when you're ready.'

'It was worthwhile reconditioning the motor.' Luke grinned. 'She runs like a dream,'

'She needed it. She's clocked up plenty of miles over the years. Appreciate you taking care of this old girl. She's the other woman in my life,' he chortled.

'Since you deal in good second hand cars, would you mind keeping an eye out for a dual cab ute. Something gutsy. Need wheels of my own and don't want to be running this beauty around the countryside too much longer.'

'Sure. I hear of anything I'll let you know.'

'Obliged.'

Then Lorraine called them in for lunch. It was a long time since Luke had known the simple privilege of sitting around a table sharing a meal with friends. Not until he'd come back to Bingun. Tilly and Stella had been the first to generously invite him and rekindle the pleasure he'd almost forgotten.

Not that Hunter meals had ever been ideal, but he was getting to like the warmth of sharing a normal routine and family life again with good people. His faith and trust in folk was starting to return.

During lunch, Lorraine nudged him with a few questions about Joe. Gossip must be running wild at the moment about the arrest but he kept his responses vague. Made it clear the man would no longer be a part of his life.

He hung around long enough to be polite, thanked Nev and Lorraine for the meal and hospitality then made his excuses, keen to head out East Road to the Meyer place the other side of town.

Despite his anticipation to finally speak to Dave, he nursed the Monaro slow and steady along the last stretch of gravel road to the farm.

Today might possibly turn out to be the biggest milestone in his life so far. He was either Dave's son or not. Only a fool would ignore the facts already learned. He was nervous and pumped to man up and face whatever reality followed.

The old Meyer homestead was a classic ornate

veranda weatherboard that had somehow survived the generations. His ancestors were one of
many hard working German farming families to
travel further north inland from the coast in the
late nineteenth century to take up land, among
the first to settle the district.

Having been raised on the land, Luke well
knew farmers depended on the seasons each year
for an income. No rain, no crops, no money. This
year, however, Dave's paddocks were looking
impressive and healthy. It promised to be a
bumper harvest which meant being busy from
November and possibly beyond Christmas. The
reason he was already lining up labour.

Probably seeing Luke's dust on the last stretch
of road and hearing the Monaro's throaty
approach, Dave was already standing at his front
house gate. Luke stepped out. The men greeted
each other with a nod, a smile and a firm
country handshake.

'Nice to see you, son. Appreciate you coming
out on short notice.'

'No problem.'

Dave nodded toward the Monaro. 'If Nev
Reed has let you drive that machine, you're a
man he can trust. You should take sense of pride
in that, son. Consider it an honour and a
compliment.'

'Thanks. I know it.'

Because Dave had always been approachable,
Luke didn't feel at all uncomfortable, only the
strain of addressing the important issue played
on his mind.

'Let's walk.' Dave indicated the track that led

off between machinery sheds toward the fence that ran around the homestead block. 'Pleased to see you back in the district.'

'It's actually good to be home,' Luke acknowledged and meant it, striding out alongside this giant humble man.

He simply sought the rural life now for the sake of it. The reason why he'd always stuck to working in the country on his travels these past few years. He liked the friendliness and familiarity of small towns.

As they passed kennels, Dave let a black and tan kelpie off its chain. 'Hey, Bruiser.' The dog wagged its tail, nuzzled his owner with affection then raced off. 'I still run sheep in the tree paddock. He's a good mate.'

They had reached the fence and each leant on a post looking out across a paddock that in the distance edged the road back to town.

'You mentioned work?' Luke prompted.

'If you're interested, son, and plan on staying, I have an offer in mind.'

'Yes to both and I'd like to hear it.'

Dave squinted and stared off toward the horizon. 'Before I pitch my proposal, there's something you need to know.' He glanced back at Luke with equally blue eyes. 'Stella came to see me a few weeks back. Told me what Joe said and that even though you tried to hide it, you were troubled. Asked me to tell you the truth one way or the other.'

Luke's heart about stopped. Stunned, he stayed silent. Dave knew! Being a straight shooter he was dealing with their personal matter first. Luke was relieved and numb. When Dave half turned away from him again, he noticed the man trying to keep his emotions under control.

'My heart died the day Alice drowned. And then you disappeared straight after Christian's funeral. Didn't know if I'd ever see you again.'

'Would that have mattered?'

'Yes, son, it surely would. But I need you to know how it was first. So you understand. You deserve to hear what your mother and I shared and how it came about.

'That first time twenty years ago when she knocked on my back door in the middle of the night before you were even born, I was shocked at the state of her. The bruises,' he scowled, shaking his head, 'and clutching Christian with such desperation. She didn't need to explain. Word gets around. I knew. Her injuries were serious enough to warrant the police but she wouldn't have it.

'I've lived alone out here, as you know. Being a big property, I don't have any neighbours close enough to see. That first night I just fed your mother and gave her one of the five spare rooms. Damn near killed me to see anyone beat up like that, especially a woman with a child.

'Next morning I pleaded one more time with Alice to report Joe but she seemed more afraid of doing that than returning to him. So I let her go. Drove her back near your farm and dropped her off so Joe didn't see. But I tell you, it was agony sending her back to that thug and doing nothing. But I couldn't break her trust. She made me promise.

'So it grew into a pattern that every so often

171

when Joe went wild again on the drink, Alice and Christian came back. We kind of got used to each other. Slid into an easy friendship. Wasn't hard. Your mother was a lovely woman. I guess we just grew closer being around each other in the house,' he nodded back toward the homestead, 'and I guess I became protective of her.

'Then one night after Joe had gone away shearing for a month, Alice started regularly coming over. Your mother always drove the back road between our two properties. We took every care. She stayed the night and left in the morning.

'Right from the first night after Christian was asleep, our conversation turned personal and a fond attraction started between us. We knew it wasn't right with Alice being married but we let our feelings take over. I swear to you, son, I always treated your mother with the respect a woman deserves. I know what we did wasn't right but I won't ever love another.'

Dave's conversation stalled awhile. Luke saw that his confession came hard, he and his mother were lovers but he hadn't actually told him in so many words what he wanted to know. The burning question still remained unanswered.

'I think I understand.'

'It was only a few weeks after Joe returned when your mother came over to tell me she was pregnant. She didn't have to say it. I saw by the shine in her eyes that I was the father. *Your* father, Luke.'

Dave faltered and looked his son straight in the eyes then reached out and instinctively grabbed him in a bear hug. Luke felt the strength

172

and warmth of a good man and in that moment knew his life had been changed forever. The weight of knowing finally lifted from his shoulders. He felt amazed and proud.

When the men pulled apart, Luke said roughly, 'Thanks for telling me.'

'The joy for us was bittersweet,' Dave went on, 'because she still wouldn't leave Joe, even knowing we loved each other. That was the hardest thing I ever had to hear and my biggest heartache and disappointment. But I've been so proud even to sit on the sidelines of your life and witness you grow up, son. And still be able to watch out for your mother and you two boys. Even though Christian wasn't my son, he would have been a welcome part of any life your mother and I may have shared if she had chosen to leave Joe.

'I would have told you sooner but your mother refused. We managed some time together over the years but our relationship in public was necessarily only friendship. As it turned out, she was right to keep the truth about you a secret.

'She did for twenty years but a few weeks before she died, Alice told me she and Joe had a serious argument. Apparently in the heat of the moment, because she had grown so fed up, she cracked and let it slip that you weren't his son. She didn't need to tell him because he never cared for either of you as a father should but she just wanted to throw something back at him that would hurt his pride.'

Dave sighed. 'It sure did. Joe exploded, started smashing things around the house. Probably

173

realised the stinging truth that he had actually lost control of his wife's love and loyalty two decades before. Alice just drove from the house to come over and warn me. We had no idea what Joe might do.

'We discussed if it was possible for her to get away from him but that you two boys would be at his mercy living and working with him on your place. I pointed out that you and Christian would always have a home with me if you wanted but, being adults, that was your decision.

'In the following weeks, after all those years Alice finally decided to leave Joe. I supported her all I could but I was worried sick about her. Knew I wouldn't rest easy until she was safely away from him and under my roof.

'By then of course Christian and Tilly were engaged and expecting a baby. During that time there were one or two unexplained *mishaps* around the farm here. An old disused hay shed burnt. Machinery tyres were mysteriously slashed. All reported and investigated but nothing was ever proved or traced back to Joe.

'Alice told me Joe went dangerously quiet after she told him about you. A few days before she died, Joe came to the farm here. He must have followed her. I met him with a rifle in one hand and a phone to call the police in the other. He tossed out cold threats but didn't stay long. At the time, we thought it seemed all too easy but, as we all know now, Joe had other plans.

'I think you know what happened soon after that and why. It's all come out recently and Joe will pay for his crimes but no prison sentence will ever be enough,' Dave said fiercely, reaching out to lay a hand on Luke's arm. 'I'm sorry, son, about your mother and brother. Nothing breaks my heart more than knowing two innocent people died at the hands of a madman out of pure spite.'

A sudden spring breeze whipped up and swept across the paddock. 'You okay, son?' Dave asked quietly.

Luke nodded. 'Appreciate your honesty and knowing what you both went through. For her own sake, I have to agree with you and wish my mother had left Joe.'

'I'm sure it's been a tough few years for you, too.'

'Damn straight,' Luke growled.

Dave straightened. 'What I've learned is to hang on tight to those memories but not look back. Future's ahead for all of us so how about coming up to the house to discuss my proposal now?'

'Sure.'

They turned and stepped out in unison. Bruiser found them again and tagged along. Luke felt strange walking beside his father and couldn't deny an aching regret that he'd known and been a part of this man's life sooner.

His life and thinking from now on would take some adjustments becoming part of another family and he hoped he lived up to their example. He also had serious plans to create a family of his own. After years of being a nomadic loner, Luke's life had been completely shaken and turned around to find a father and the woman he loved within weeks of coming home.

Inside the Meyer homestead, Dave introduced him to a wall of ancestral photos. Then wandered briefly through the big old rambling house, clearly built for the needs of a large immigrant family. It was a lot to take in but they soon settled down in comfortable chairs to celebrate their new relationship with beers.

'I'll get straight to the point, Luke. I've had plenty of time over the years to think on it. I'm a bachelor. You're my only son. I bought out my two sisters' share of the farm years ago but I still have a niggling mortgage I'd like to reduce. I know you're driving grain at the moment but my offer is to come and work with me in partnership here on the farm full time if you're interested and you can see that as your future.

'After all we've discussed today, you'll want to take your time and think on it. It's a new situation for both of us and I won't pressure you at all. Either way, this house and property,' he glanced around, 'will be yours one day through rightful inheritance.'

Hell. Luke leaned forward and almost spilled his drink. This place was thousands of hectares.

'Don't panic,' Dave grinned. 'Just feel free to drop in any time and visit. You have an open invitation to get to know me and at my age, I could sure use the permanent help. But, like I said, no pressure, son. And don't worry about the family. A few years back we had a round table conference so my sisters, Lizzie and Helen, have been generously compensated for their share of the farm.

'None of my nieces or nephews want to be farmers but they do love to come visit their old bachelor uncle from time to time so you'll get acquainted with them all.' He sat forward in his chair and leaned across, extending his arm. 'So do we have a deal you'll think it over?'

Luke's mind was spinning with information but he had no hesitation in shaking hands on it. A gentleman's agreement and time to decide. He liked that. Their grip was firm and sure.

After he stopped off at Nev's garage to get the Monaro checked on his way home, he needed to speak to Tilly real bad.

14

Nev had wanted a chin wag after working on the Monaro but Luke was impatient to leave and didn't stay long. When he finally arrived back at the farmhouse, Tilly was perched on the top step, her arms hugging her knees

Her smile lit up her face as he pulled up. She would have not only seen his dust but in the classic machine he was driving, would have heard his approach, too, so she was already leaping down and at the vehicle before he had barely stopped.

'Hey,' she whispered when he cut the engine and opened the door.

He stepped out, wrapped his arms around her waist and kissed her hard awhile, needing the emotional release. They pulled apart and she tossed him an expectant glance. Luke was still processing his conversation with Dave together with its potential outcome and ripple effect on his life but it had come time to actually tell someone.

While he hesitated, Tilly frowned, 'Did he say?'

Luke nodded.

When he stayed silent and just stood there poker-faced, she punched him lightly on the arm. 'Don't tease.' Her caring and uncertainty on his behalf were endearing. 'Do you want to share?'

He nodded again.

'So . . . yes or no?'

He leaned in real close again, brushed aside strands of long soft hair from her ear and breathed, 'Yes.'

With a sharp gasp, she leaned back and clutched his arms. 'It was true!' A pause while she watched him. 'How do you feel about that?'

If he hadn't returned to Bingun, renewed his friendship with Tilly and their previous friendship had not bloomed into a connection way more than he could ever have hoped and prayed for, he would have had absolutely no one to share this moment. Deep in his gut he knew he wouldn't have wanted it to be anyone else.

'Strange. But overwhelmed. In a good way.'

Tilly let out a light squeal and hugged him around his neck in an amazingly fierce grip. The woman looked lean but she sure had plenty of strength in those arms. And he didn't mind a bit. Just held her tight, breathing in the fresh country scent of her — a hint of lavender maybe — and stood there super content with his life right now and being loved.

They hadn't said the words yet to each other but the strong chemistry and feelings were there, growing deeper every day. No question.

He suspected both of them, because of other family concerns on their minds right now, were holding back until time and fate played them out and their lives were more settled again. For Tilly, he knew that meant dealing with Stella's failing health and her forthcoming grief. For himself, it was wanting to develop an understanding and

179

bond with his natural father while considering the direction of his future.

Damn straight he wanted Tilly to be a part of it. For now though, they could only continue to support each other and push through their troubles together.

When they broke apart, Tilly led Luke to the front steps where they sat and watched the sharp evening light stripe gum tree shadows across the long entrance driveway and the lush grasses beneath the stands of trees dotting the surrounding house paddock. Maturing crops spread to the horizon, ripening in the warming spring sun ahead of another harvest season.

When his brain focused again, Luke asked, 'How's your Ma?'

'Having a rest. Recovering.'

'It's been a big day.'

'Mmm. Ma seems . . . peaceful now. In an eerie way. I guess I should be happy for her but it worries me. Makes me fearful. I know what's coming for her but now it's like she's found acceptance and is even willing it all to end. It's frightening.' Tilly shivered and Luke reached for her hands. She turned to him with deep affection in her eyes in response to his comforting gesture and went on, 'You'll have heaps to think about, too, after seeing Dave.'

'At first I didn't know what to think. He described how his relationship and feelings for Mum developed. I found it hard to accept her tolerance of Joe's mistreatment and that she was unfaithful with another man. Even if he was to be my father. On the surface, their affair might sound seedy but once Dave explained how it happened and seeing him for the decent man he is, I find it hard to judge and lay blame. Mum sought him out for genuine reasons. It was fate that they found comfort and pleasure together.'

'Knowing both of them,' Tilly offered softly, 'admittedly Dave from a distance really, but Alice through being Ma's best friend, and keeping in mind both of their individual circumstances — Dave's loneliness and your mother's unhappiness — you couldn't deny them true love. Their lives drew them together into a secret liaison. I'm glad they found each other,' she ended firmly.

Luke smiled and hugged her closer. All things considered, he was inclined to agree. 'As I left Dave's place earlier, he mentioned another option to consider a ways down the track. He said if I agree and decide to jump on board with him in a farming partnership, he would be humbled if I'd give thought to the possibility of legally taking up the Meyer surname.'

'Really! What do you think?'

'You know what, it would be an honour,' Luke murmured. 'I feel a kind of empty sadness and the deepest regret that Joe got to be the figurehead in my life so far. That's probably the biggest disappointment I can find in my mother's thinking. But then again Chris and I were close brothers. Maybe she figured that bond might be broken if she told me. It's a huge admission to make at any time in a person's life.'

He pushed out a heavy sigh. 'Once I've adjusted to my new situation, assuming I go ahead with the partnership offer, I believe the name change thing will help me personally and confirm to Dave my respect for him and my true family heritage.

'You know,' he clenched his jaw, trying to stem his rising emotions, 'naturally I wish my mother was still alive but even more so after what Dave confided today. We could have been a real family. Sounds like we came close, but for Joe.'

Tilly groaned. 'This year has been a game changer, huh?'

Luke squeezed her hand. Tragic for her, better for him. Life swung like the wind and they both had experience of learning to cope.

'You already know peace comes with time and acceptance. I wish that for you again,' he murmured.

'Thank you,' she whispered and tilted her face up to be kissed.

He obliged.

'Sounds like you'll be farming on the Meyer place. What will happen to Joe's farm?'

Luke shrugged. 'No idea and don't care but it would be a shame to see the property abandoned and deteriorate. I want nothing to do with it and Joe sure wouldn't want me to set foot on it. Suits me fine. I guess rates will accumulate. Might drop in to the shire office and see what can be done.'

'Want to join us for dinner?' Tilly offered.

'You know what, thanks, but I'm gonna take some time out tonight. Have an early grain run down to Portland again tomorrow.'

'Sure.'

Tilly stretched and rose as the last of the sun's

rays brought twilight over the land and the tranquillity of another approaching night. As they talked, the roos had come out of the bush to feed, some still grazing lower down in the house paddock.

'See you tomorrow night, then?' Tilly cheekily turned her body into his when he stood up too.

'It's a date,' he murmured, her soft curves and warmth a definite turn-on.

A last lingering spicy kiss sealed the deal, every single one they shared now harder to break and not take further.

★ ★ ★

Although she stubbornly hoped otherwise, Tilly's unwanted instinct was right. As the week progressed and within days of her celebration of life service, as if her body knew her task was done, Stella's health rapidly declined.

On leave from teaching, caring for her Ma night and day, Tilly operated on automatic. She didn't let herself stop and think. Just did what needed to be done. Luke became her quiet supportive backstop. Gone early truck driving every day but by her side each evening, instinctively knowing she just needed him around.

With the late spring heat burning the paddocks of dense green to golden brown, he had already spoken to the grain company, arranging to work for Dave during harvest, possibly continuing his driving in the New Year.

For Tilly, the usual Christmas festivities ahead were an ordeal she already planned to ignore.

But as Stella weakened, it came time to phone Doctor Singh who was at the farmhouse door within fifteen minutes. Although the district nurse had started calling in daily to check on Stella and bolster Tilly's flagging spirits, the doctor gently recommended her mother be transferred to Horsham hospital.

With every stubborn fibre in her body, Tilly had resisted this moment. Ma leaving the farm for the last time felt wrong. Cruel. She had spent her life creating and tending a massively productive market garden and orchard, already heavy with the new season's produce.

Tilly had grasped the opportunity to take charge of the outdoor work, a breather from the distressing mood indoors. But still checked on her Ma every half hour, bringing in the latest fruit and vegetable pickings or bunch of flowers from the garden. Tilly took endless photos on her phone so Stella could see the rewards of her efforts that her daughter was merely reaping.

The weak smile of pleasure, all that Stella could manage, was the only gratitude Tilly needed.

So it was with a heavy reluctant heart she watched her mother being wheeled into the ambulance. She left a note on the cottage table for Luke, hastily stuffed a change of clothes and toiletries into a small overnight bag and drove numbly behind the emergency vehicle. Later, she aimlessly paced the hospital corridors while her mother was assessed and admitted into a ward.

Luke phoned. In the country, a half hour drive to anywhere was nothing but because it was a weekday and his work start and loading were often still in the dark, she assured him she would be fine and keep in touch. She knew he wanted to be there for her but there was little to be done.

She booked into an apartment overlooking the central park where she quickly dashed under a shower, returning to the hospital within the hour. For the next two days, she sat by Stella's bedside all day and well into the night. She ate hospital food and watched and waited and read.

Friday evening, although long past visiting hours, shuffling in the hallway alerted her to another presence.

Luke.

Wearily, she rose from her chair and melted into his arms. He had flowers and a soft smile of concern. No words. They didn't need them.

'These are for you.'

'Thanks.'

They snatched a fleeting warm kiss of longing that Tilly ached to become so much more but staff bustled in and out. Impossible to be passionate and she was exhausted anyway. Luke pulled up a chair and they sat by Stella's bedside. Her mother had grown pale, mostly dozing with medication, her usually wild grey hair limp now.

Stella Schroder passed peacefully the following night. The end of life as Tilly had known it for the last three years since her father died and the two women had rubbed on alone so harmoniously together.

How could she go on?

Life suddenly felt useless and desolate.

Ghost-like, Tilly drifted through each day. On

compassionate leave and not yet back at school for fourth term, she was lost. Grief-stricken at this last severed family tie she had so uselessly battled.

Luke still drove the grain trucks but when he wasn't working or supporting Tilly, could be found across town on Dave Meyer's farm helping him prepare for harvest.

Locals and neighbours called in to the Schroder place. No one knocked. They just all tramped across the veranda and let themselves in through the kitchen door bringing enough food for the fridge and freezer that Tilly wouldn't need to cook for weeks. A forest of perfumed flowers filled the farmhouse, cards stacked two deep along the mantelpiece. Most folk simply said a kind word, warmly remarked on Stella's memorable celebration of life service and left.

At night, Luke slept in the spare room, Tilly grateful he was close. Much as she loved her home, for the moment she didn't care to be in the house alone.

The funeral five days later was a small family affair and Tilly was thankful for the privacy. At Luke's request and with her implicit approval, Dave Meyer stood on the other side of his son. It tugged at Tilly's heart in the loveliest way to see them standing together looking so much alike.

As if she hadn't cried enough tears alone, Tilly was securely held as Pastor conducted the brief ceremony with prayers at the same graveside where she had farewelled her father three years before, and her fiancé and baby daughter two years before that. With Luke's strong arm firmly around her shoulders, hugging her tight against him, his strength was significant.

Within days of the funeral, a suit from the agricultural company that leased the farm, stood like another grim reaper under the veranda. Tilly knew why and invited him in. She patiently listened to his pitch and said no. Fair enough his big company was a business but his timing sucked and she let him know it.

Bingun and this farm were home and she planned to stay. Like many farmers hereabouts she was property rich and cash poor but what use was over a million dollars if you were homeless? Where else would she go?

Sure, in the light of family tragedies in recent years, it might be considered heartbreak country but those sorrows eased. She loved her town's charm and village atmosphere. The Wimmera was in her blood. Its breezes caressed her soul. Her heart and spirit belonged here.

In the following weeks, owing to Tilly's strong urge to visit and chat to her mother, Stella's fresh grave always brimmed with flowers. When her grief grew overwhelming, she grabbed a handful of her Ma's gardening clothes and buried her face in them to quietly weep. All the while she felt Luke's blue eyes silently watching her. His life was on track, hers had taken a temporary slide downhill.

She knew the gloom would ease but, when the empty loneliness became a burden, even with Luke around, she took herself in hand, put herself out into public life again and returned to teaching for the last weeks of school.

She wished she had done it sooner. The children were a tonic and blessing who stirred her spirits with the extra excitement, at least for them, of Christmas in the air. So Tilly forced herself to appear enthusiastic.

With the distraction of routine came a certain level of peace so that by harvest Luke caught her full attention again. The rumble of headers was already beating up and down the paddocks around the farm. Besides keeping up with garden watering, Tilly also kept the fridge and freezer stocked with food and cold drinks for the men's lunch eskies.

Luke was mostly absent working with Dave on the other side of town. When he did appear tired and dusty at random intervals, invitation laced the mildest touches and covert glances. Her body hummed with pleasure whether he was in her thoughts or around her in person.

She sensed a returning leashed energy in his every lean muscled movement and barely controlled fire in his kisses and hands that fanned the flames in her own body. Which, not only to Tilly's frustration, she noticed, neither of them were able to explore until after harvest while the focus was full power ahead on getting the year's bounty into the silos.

The men worked flat out every day in shifts and, depending on the temperature overnight, often after sunset and on into the dark of hot nights.

Christmas, when it snuck up, was a quiet acknowledgement of the season with just Luke and Dave invited to the farmhouse exchanging simple gifts and then indulging in one big tender

188

turkey roast and plum pudding lunch despite the heat.

Dave left mid-afternoon to visit his sisters and their families up country for a few days. The surrounding stubble paddocks and dusty browning landscape signalled the onslaught of high summer to come.

With no school on her schedule for six weeks, another year ending and a new one about to begin, Tilly's thoughts of her future beckoned, rising to the forefront of her mind. She understood that Luke was leaving it up to her to let him know when she was ready. He was having trouble holding back but while she knew he would wait, she was also gasping with a desperate need to express her love in the most intimate way.

So as she and Luke sat out on the veranda steps after dark as usual one night, with crickets singing their usual chorus and the summer night's still heat settling around them, their quiet country world lit by brilliant stars, she knew it was time to make a move.

Only problem, there was an unknown factor in the mix she needed to explain. She could only hope he would understand. The complication had hovered like an unwanted phantom in the back of her mind as she gradually fell in love with Luke. She hadn't wanted to say anything until their love was firm and their future together more certain.

Now when it came time to tell him, she could only pray at this late stage that it wasn't a deal breaker for any future relationship.

15

Tilly drew courage and a deep breath to speak. 'Luke — '

'Tilly — '

They exchanged wry grins. Seems they both had similar thoughts in mind.

'Go for it,' he said.

Tilly was relieved. Before Luke said anything she needed to talk first. 'To be honest, even as teenagers, I knew you liked me and I thought you were cute but — '

'You couldn't take your eyes off my big brother.'

'True,' she confessed, smiling, 'but Christian's not here with us anymore. As a fiancé or a brother. We both lost him, Luke, not just me.' She fiddled uncomfortably. 'It's taken a while but since you've returned, the last ties to that part of my past have slid away. I'm not only ready to move on now, I want to.' She pushed out a heavy breath. 'Moving on. I hate that phrase. Like you can up and leave memories and people behind that we've loved and lost. You don't just snap your fingers and forget.'

She turned to Luke and her voice softened with affection. 'I wouldn't have you if I hadn't loved and lost Chris. That episode has shaped who I am now. Neither of us is the same person we were five years ago. So I'm not so much ready to move on, Luke, I want to move forward with you. There's a difference. I want to laugh and smile again. And I can. Because I love you,' she ended on a passionate whisper.

They reached for each other and Luke gathered her into his arms. 'I love you back, Tilly. Always have, always will. You had my heart a long time ago. You've made my wildest dream come true. No matter what, I can't imagine my life without you.'

He hesitated, deep adoration shining out of those too blue eyes and his deep honest gaze. For a moment, Tilly panicked. She sensed what he might be about to say. This was all happening so suddenly and fast, both of them swept away by the heady freedom of finally admitting their love. They wanted each other so badly. Luke was so hard to resist.

Ignoring the fact that she hadn't told him yet and washed with an overwhelming hunger for this country man who had quietly entered her life again, infiltrated her heart and stolen it completely, she closed her eyes and allowed herself to be drawn against him, craved the feel of strong arms, the slight roughness of stubble on his face, the sexy fullness of his mouth which was suddenly on hers. Just this one, then she would tell him.

She set aside the feeling of guilt she hid deep down as the kiss started tender, exploratory and demanding, then hurtled toward passion. Luke hauled her by long tanned legs until her shapely bottom in shorts was perched in his lap so they faced each other. She slid her arms around his hot sun browned body and let her hands weave their way into his thick hair, tugging him close.

His rough warm farmer's hands pushed up beneath her sleeveless tank top and began to explore, working their way to the front to cover her bare breasts. She knew it was cheeky but nature had been unashamedly generous to her. In the isolation of living in the country on a farm and especially in the heat, she saw no need to hide her assets which Luke now caressed with reverent appreciation.

She gasped as the kiss grew hot and heavy, her need urgent and explosive. Before they gave in to their raging appetite for each other, Tilly moaned. Languid with passion, she somehow found the strength to press her hand against Luke's shirt and pull back.

He raised his sandy eyebrows in hope. 'Inside?'

Tilly swallowed. 'Hold that thought. Something I need to tell you first.'

Luke frowned. 'Sounds serious.'

She slid from his lap and sat alongside again so she didn't have to look at him, her hands clenched together, feeling tense and miserable. Stella had known, of course, but she had never told anyone else nor needed to. Until now. So she just jumped in and began.

'The night of the crash when Chris was killed and my caesarean to birth Anna May revealed she hadn't survived the trauma, I was in a bad way. The reason I was in hospital so long and I couldn't attend his funeral was because of further complications. I had severe internal injuries and was bleeding heavily so because my life was in danger, the surgeon had no choice but to perform a hysterectomy.'

Tilly stopped. Luke would know what that meant now but she needed to voice it.

'I can't have children.'

She sensed movement beside her but he said nothing. When she dared glance at him his face was stricken with a deep agony before he leaned forward and sank his head into his hands, elbows on his knees.

Her worse fears were realised. He was taking it hard. She knew her timing was lousy but there never would have been a right or better moment. Certainly not just after they both floated high and had been about to ravish each other.

Tilly didn't dare reach out and touch him. 'You're disappointed. I'll understand if — '

'Hell no.' Luke rasped out and swung around to face her. 'I'm so sorry. I'll always feel responsible for getting drunk that night and being the catalyst for Chris sitting in the driver's seat of my car.'

Tilly's whole body sank with relief and she took a deep breath to stem a happy sob. He didn't care. He still wanted her but was wrongly loading guilt onto his own shoulders.

'Don't go there. You're not to blame. Joe is and he's finally being punished.' She took a moment before she continued. 'Sure, it hurts that I can't have babies. I've had a few years to adjust my thinking on it. Families take on all forms. Look at you and Dave now. Who knew? He's already becoming an important part of your life. We all have to adapt to what life throws at us but, for what it's worth, I'm just aching and ready to foster or adopt some kids.'

Luke shook his head and his face spread into a lazy larrikin smile. 'More than one, huh?'

'Well, while we're on a roll I wouldn't want to stop. There are so many needy children out there just waiting to find a home.'

'Whatever you want, I'm on board.'

'So, you still want me?' she asked humbly, blushing.

'Tilly Schroder,' he growled, 'you have no idea how much.'

She laughed and edged closer, craving the contact. 'Oh I think I'm beginning to get an idea,' she purred, slowly shaking her head, 'I feel so damn lucky to know love again. Christian will always hold a place in a corner of my heart but I'm in love with you now, Luke,' she whispered, 'for the good man you are. You're so much more than a country boy with boots, a hat and a swagger. You have a big generous heart, a deep conscience, and a sense of right and wrong. Principles you inherited from Alice and Dave.'

'You're making me feel mighty humble Matilda Schroder and damn happy that you love me back.'

'Well Ma told me once that happiness often sneaks in a door we didn't even know was open,' she grinned, adding in a whisper, 'I'm sorry you had to wait but fate wasn't ready for us to be together.'

'You take my breath away,' he whispered back. 'You've been a farmer's daughter. Could you be a farmer's wife?'

Sitting right beside her looking gorgeous and

irresistible and uncertain, Luke waited for her answer. She had known for a long time what that would be.

'Reckon I could give it a good old Schroder try.'

She slid her arms around his waist until their lips were a breath apart. 'I like you and me the way we are. We like Bingun. Dave's living on his farm. I'm all alone here.' She flashed a cheeky pout and he chuckled. Tilly half turned to look back toward the farmhouse. 'This place doesn't have any bad memories. No mortgage. We could keep the land leased out or work it ourselves and you'll be share farming with Dave.'

He shrugged and drawled, 'Can't argue with that logic,' slowly rising to stand and starting to pop the buttons on his shirt.

Tilly fanned herself in fake surprise and stood to face him. 'Did I expect you to stay decent?'

'Hope not.' He finished the shirt and shrugged it off.

Her gaze flickered with approval over acres of summer-brown bare chest. 'A girl can never have too much of a good thing,' she murmured, unzipping her denim shorts and peeling them down her legs.

Groaning with impatience, he grabbed her and their bodies collided all the way down, generous soft curves and bulges fitting nicely together.

Since both of them were half undressed anyway, Tilly gasped, 'Hell if you don't make love to me soon I'll faint. Course on the up side that could involve falling into your arms.'

'Where you belong.'

Tilly shrieked. In one powerful movement, a pair of big strong farmer's arms swept her up and into the house.

We do hope that you have enjoyed reading this large print book.

Did you know that all of our titles are available for purchase?

We publish a wide range of high quality large print books including:
Romances, Mysteries, Classics
General Fiction
Non Fiction and Westerns

Special interest titles available in large print are:
The Little Oxford Dictionary
Music Book
Song Book
Hymn Book
Service Book

Also available from us courtesy of Oxford University Press:
Young Readers' Dictionary
(large print edition)
Young Readers' Thesaurus
(large print edition)

For further information or a free brochure, please contact us at:
Ulverscroft Large Print Books Ltd.,
The Green, Bradgate Road, Anstey,
Leicester, LE7 7FU, England.
Tel: (00 44) 0116 236 4325
Fax: (00 44) 0116 234 0205

Other titles published by Ulverscroft:

FOSSICKER'S GULLY

Noelene Jenkinson

When journalist Amy Randall is abducted at gunpoint by her sister-in-law, Kelly, and left in an old mine tunnel to die, she is lucky to escape. Allowing Kelly to believe her sinister plan has succeeded, Amy goes into hiding to investigate. Local policeman Alex Hammond, her childhood crush and her brother's lifelong friend, agrees to help, and offers Amy a place to stay at his flat. What is Kelly hiding, and why does she seem bent on revenge against the Randall family? It's a race to uncover the truth before Kelly finds a new victim, and meanwhile, Amy and Alex draw closer. Set in a small town in the central Victorian gold-fields, *Fossicker's Gully* throws old friends together, brings new love, and reveals a heart-warming family secret.